A Band of Gold

Patricia N. Richards

VANTAGE PRESS
New York

This is a work of fiction. Any similarity between the names
and characters in this book and any real persons, living or
dead, is purely coincidental.

Cover design by Polly McQuillen

FIRST EDITION

Copyright © 2008 by Patricia N. Richards

Published by Vantage Press, Inc.
419 Park Ave. South, New York, NY 10016

Manufactured in the United States of America
ISBN: 978-0-533-15791-4

Library of Congress Catalog Card No.: 2007903020

0 9 8 7 6 5 4 3 2 1

To my husband, Jim,
and our two daughters, Teresa and Linda

Prologue

Brilliant colors of corals and golds become engulfed in the deep blue of the darkened night. Stars sparkle like gems, while they liven up the heavens. In the quiet of such an evening one can dream away the uncertainties of the day. Of course not everyone notices God's resplendent beauty of a sunset, especially on such an overwhelming day on a ranch several miles from a small northwestern town known as Cascadia in the territory of Washington.

This was an inevitable hour of mourning in the McCalister home. After several months of suffering, Matilda McCalister's lifeless body lay resting at peace under a huge maple tree on a hill overlooking the McCalister ranch. Joel McCalister stood grief-stricken under the massive maple by his wife's grave, reflecting on memories of years gone by; in many ways it seemed like only yesterday.

His Mattie was very lovely, with eyes the color of sapphire, fair complexion and long, shiny dark hair often worn with a ribbon at the nape of her neck. She was not a large woman, but had been toughened by life's adversities and had developed a self-reliant posture.

Joel and Mattie had discussed moving out west many times, something almost unheard of in their day. Usually the husband made a decision and the spouse had to abide by it. Not with Joel. He and Mattie always shared their plans and dreams, and together came to an agreement.

Finally, the day had arrived when their secret dream became reality. Their plans were finalized to join a wagon train and become a part of the adventure of settling a land yet untamed out west. With a large part of the money received from the sale of their small farm, they purchased a wagon, a team of oxen and all the supplies they had been told would be needed for the hazardous journey. Oxen, they soon learned, were the best animals to pull a wagon. The husky animals cost less money, adapted much better to the dry prairie grasses, and the Indians found them less of an attraction than a horse or a mule for stealing. Many times they discovered families would become so attached to their oxen they would grieve, if the animal were to die. The McCalisters' small covered wagon had been loaded with as many supplies and very special possessions as they could find a space to place them.

Joel recalled Mattie surveying the humble but comfortable home they would be leaving behind. Mattie had tried to discourage the butterflies that had begun stirring up her stomach; the move west became both stimulating, and to a degree, frightening to her. Joel reminisced the comments of relatives and friends. Some shared their excitement and wished to be going along; others tried to discourage them by mentioning how foolish they were to leave a comfortable home, friends, and loved ones for a life of hardship in a wilderness they knew so little about.

But Joel and Mattie were fascinated to become a part of the growing west; being pioneers encouraged their determination. With a deep love for each other and a strong devotion to God, and their small son, Thomas, they each believed their faith would be strengthened and any hardships which might challenge them would be overcome.

As Mattie stood looking over their abandoned home, her eyes had settled on a little twig of a tree. Joel smiled as he remembered her plea: "Oh, Joel, let's take it with us! Maybe there won't be any maple trees in the west, and I think one of the things I would miss most would be a maple tree. I love the trees in the fall, when the leaves change to brilliant colors. In the winter after the leaves have fallen the limbs appear lonely and dead. But then spring comes with its magnificent splendor, and new buds once again become triumphant and proclaim to the world, 'I'm alive and will challenge the world again.' "

"But Mattie, I'm sure there must be maples out west," he had tried to discourage her.

"Joel, please! Let's take it with us," she had pleaded.

"All right, Mattie. We'll take the sprig." Refusing his lovely bride anything was always hard on him to do. "Be sure to get plenty of root and soil. Here, put it in this old barrel so you can keep it watered well. For your sake I'll hope it survives," he remembered saying.

Movement west had been gradual until the California Gold Rush had infiltrated the news, resulting in gold fever, which inspired visionaries to travel westward. The trip had been strenuous as they had been warned. Each of the travelers had to submit to numerous sacrifices. There were unfamiliar diseases, marauding Indians, in many places a lack of water. Travel, often harsh, slow, and dangerous due to the poor trails, encouraged yet another river to cross, another rugged mountain to climb. Numbers of families had faced the sting of death, causing spirits to become low. But, eventually, someone with a cheerful outlook would happen along to encourage and brighten up the venture.

Some travelers journeyed west to seek their fortune. A number were running away from the law. Many had aspirations of fulfilling a dream of adventure and a new life. Unfortunately, the Indian uprisings discouraged many people. Among the most tragic was the Whitman Massacre in 1847.

Joel recalled the Eastern newspapers reporting the story of Dr. Marcus Whitman. Along with his new bride, Narcissa, the doctor had started a mission along the Oregon Trail at Walla Walla in the Territory of Washington in 1836. The mission became an important station for other emigrants as well as a medical center. They had succeeded in converting many Indians to the Christian Faith, and helping them in numerous ways. The newspapers stated that Dr. Whitman had been out the previous night of the massacre attending sick patients, only to come home to a house full of sick people. A Cayuse chief, who had been clothed, cared for, and befriended by Dr. Whitman, was the leader of a small band of Indian attackers arriving that dreadful night. While one Indian began striking up a conversation with the unsuspecting doctor, the chief struck him in the head with his tomahawk. Mrs. Whitman ran to the aid of her husband and tried dragging him into the living room. But, she too, was shot in the chest. The renegades then dragged her outside, where they shot the wounded Narcissa several more times.

The missionaries had been well-known in the Washington and Oregon Territories. The Whitmans had accommodated travelers passing through, and worked with the Indians for eleven years, only to end their efforts in such a grievous violence. In all, fourteen people had been found murdered that evening, and fifty women and children taken as prisoners. It was a custom for the Indians to use their captives as slaves. When the terrible crime was brought to the attention of Territorial Chief Factor, Peter Ogden, he quickly assembled together enough goods to buy back every prisoner from their captors in only a month's time following the massacre.

Trying to make some sense out of the tragedy, it was decided that several reasons led to the uprising. After the Catholic missionaries arrived in the area the Indians had noticed antagonism between the religions of the Protestants and Catholics, which seemed confusing to them; also, the Indians resented the pale faces coming in, taking over their land, bringing with them a contagious disease, the measles, which killed half of the Cayuse tribe. The Indians blamed the Whitmans; because the doctor's medicine helped the white children get well, but not theirs. Many of the Cayuse felt they were being poisoned in an effort to make way for the white emigrants.

Later, in 1850, the Oregon Donation Act granted three hundred and twenty acres to every man who would settle and live on the land, and his wife was to receive the same amount. This still was done without any concern for the Indian.

It was the year 1853 when the young McCalisters had settled in the northern section of the Oregon Territory. The McCalisters were granted six hundred forty acres of land west of the Cascade Range of mountains, settled it, and through many trials and sacrifices, came to love this wild, undeveloped country. They were blessed with three fine sons. Thomas was now a man of twenty-six; Paul, twenty-three; and Mark, twenty-one.

Mark had been away studying to become a doctor in the footsteps of his hero, Dr. Marcus Whitman, at Whitman College in Walla Walla east of the mountains, until he received word of his mother's serious illness. The rugged terrain of the Cascade mountains made travel slow. Mark arrived home only a few days before his mother's death.

The doctor who attended Mattie had explained to the McCalisters that she had Hodgkin's Disease, and ailment involving the lymph glands. Mattie's trouble may have started by an infection of her tonsils, and then spread to her lymph glands. Dr. Rider stated, in Mrs. McCalister's case, the bone marrow had become affected, causing a secondary anemia. By the time Joel was able to reach the doctor the disease had spread to her spinal cord; this caused the lower part of her body to become paralyzed. The doctor had to give Mrs. McCalister a blood transfusion out of necessity. At this time blood transfusions were extremely dangerous. Mattie, though a brave, strong willed woman, just didn't have the stamina to fight off the disease.

As Joel stood, slumped from fatigue and inner suffering under the maple, Mattie's maple, he brought to mind again the doctor's words, ". . . by the time Joel was able to reach a doctor . . . Mrs. McCalister was a brave, strong-willed woman . . . just didn't have any more strength to fight . . ."

How well he knew the urgent need for doctors in the west. Individual families had to rely on their own medications and provincial knowledge much of the time. Mark had been studying to be a doctor. This year's studies were interrupted now, and he wouldn't start his travel back across the Cascades until late summer to resume his education.

These remembrances were plaguing on the mind of Joel McCalister, while he lingered just a few more minutes under the large maple tree his devoted wife had planted and loved so dearly.

One

Limited conversation could be heard from the four men seated around the supper table, as the sun finished its descent behind the snowcapped mountains. Sarah Judson had prepared a light supper for them, but even at that, much remained untouched. The Judsons were the closest neighbors, their farm being nearly three miles down the road from the McCalister ranch. A great deal of Sarah's time had been donated in helping out at the McCalisters' home after Mattie became ill. Sarah, a lovely girl with long blond hair, blue eyes and a dearness about her was eighteen, the oldest of ten children, and accustomed to helping her mother with household chores.

The neighing of horses in the nearby corral interrupted the reserved silence. "The horses appear to be a little restless tonight, Pa. I'd better see if I can calm them down," remarked the elder son, Tom.

"Sure, son. I reckon we're all a little uneasy tonight," agreed the father.

Only a short time later they were all startled to find Tom struggling with a small figure as he pushed through the door. The figure appeared to be a young boy, if he would only hold still long enough for them to distinguish. Tom was having quite a struggle restraining the little varmint's body, in between kicks.

"Well, now, what do we have here?" exclaimed the frowning Joel.

7

"I found this rascal trying to steal one of our horses," replied Tom, a little out of breath and somewhat annoyed from the contention.

"Okay, son, what's your name?" The older man paused long enough to give the intruder time to answer. "Hmm, not very talkative are you? Would you like to give us a reason for trying to steal our horse?" Joel questioned in a calm, but stern manner.

The lad finally stopped kicking, but kept his head turned downward as if ashamed, yet still squirming a bit. "Son, I reckon the lad is hungry." Joel couldn't help but notice the dirty, smelly, ragged clothes. "You'd better get him cleaned up. Maybe he'll be ready to explain his actions after having a bite to eat."

Suddenly the youth broke loose and ran towards the door. Tom and Paul grabbed for the lad, nearly pulling off his jacket. In the struggle his hat fell to the floor. It was then the men's astonished eyes noticed a long dark lock of auburn-colored hair fall down the shoulders of the distraught victim.

"Well, I'll be! That's not a boy, it's a girl!" exclaimed Paul. The other men's mouths had nearly dropped to the floor.

Fear showed in somber eyes of despair of the trapped intruder; tears began to flow down her cheeks, and then she collapsed to the floor. Tom quickly picked the small frame up and carried her gently to the couch. Her soiled threadbare clothing reeked of a disagreeable odor, and was torn in several places. Splotches of mud concealed much of her features. It was obvious her long, straggly hair hadn't seen a comb for quite some time.

"I wonder what she really looks like when she's cleaned up," Mark grinned.

"Say, Mark, why don't you ride into town for the doctor?

It appears she's going to need some attention when she comes to," advised Joel.

"Doc Rider told us yesterday that he would be leaving on the stage for Naches right after the funeral, and wouldn't be back for a couple of days," Sarah interrupted after hearing all the commotion. She was in the kitchen washing dishes, and had come to investigate.

"A good scrubbin', a night of rest, and some nourishing food would probably be the best medicine right now anyway. Sarah, do you suppose your folks would mind if you spend the night here? It probably would make it somewhat easier on the young lady if you are present when she awakes," said Joel.

"Mama already told me it would be all right to spend a day or two, if I would be of any help after the funeral, so they don't really expect me home tonight anyway."

"Fine then," said Joel. "We'd better get this girl cleaned up and into bed. You girls can share the guest room downstairs."

It had been a lengthy, stressful day. A good night's rest would be a relief for all concerned.

An early morning found Sarah busy in the well-stocked kitchen preparing a hearty breakfast for four hungry men; indeed the bacon, eggs, pile of biscuits and gravy set off the taste buds, as she placed the food on the table when the men sat down to eat.

"How did our guest sleep last night?" the older man asked.

"I don't think she changed positions all night. She was still sleeping like an infant when I got up this morning. She must have been just plain exhausted," Sarah answered.

"I wonder who she is," Paul thought out loud. "I don't recognize her from around this area."

"From the looks of her torn clothes and caked-on mud, it appears she had been traveling for days," suggested Tom.

"When she wakes up, maybe we can get some information out of her. Sarah, would you keep a close watch on the girl? This will be a strange place to her, and it may be frightening when she awakens."

"Of course I will, Mr. McCalister."

"Oh, Mark, would you let Mama know I'll be staying her for a few more days and have her pack a few of my things? The girl looks about my size. Perhaps she could fit into some of my clothes."

"Sure. Will do. See you all later," Mark waved as he left the room.

The girl didn't waken until later that evening. Sarah had spent most of the day near her bedside. She managed to find some mending to do, helping to pass the time. As the small frame began to stir, Sarah glanced up from her sewing. The girl's eyes opened rather drowsily at first, appearing to be in a daze. She surveyed the room very slowly, looking confused while trying to take everything in. All of a sudden she rose up quickly, then fell back against the pillow.

"You'd better take it a little easier," remarked Sarah with a kind smile.

"Who . . . who are you? Where am I? What am I doing here?"

"I'm Sarah Judson. You are in the guest room of the McCalister family. Don't you remember what you were doing here last night?"

"Well, well. I thought I heard voices coming from this room. So you finally decided to join the living," began Mr. McCalister cheerfully, as he knocked on the slightly opened door. "My name is Joel McCalister, and what might we call you?"

The frightened eyes appeared to soften a mite when she noticed the elder McCalister's smile.

"My . . . ah . . . my name?" The girl displayed a look of puzzlement on her face. "I . . . I don't know. Everything seems so strange." Her body began to quiver.

"Just take it easy now, little lady. There's no need to be alarmed. You don't have to answer a lot of questions just yet. Sarah, is there some broth in the kitchen? I imagine this young lady could use a bit of nourishment, then we'll talk some more."

"Yes, sir. I made some this morning. I'll be right back."

Quite evident, the girl was famished, when she picked the bowl up in her hands, and gulped down the broth. After finishing the soup, it wasn't long till the family gathered around her bed.

"Are you too tired to talk, dear?" asked Joel.

"No...no. I feel much better now. Thanks." A smile gingerly spread across her face before she realized, then it quickly disappeared.

"First, I would like you to meet my sons. Tom, Paul and Mark," he pointed individually to each of the men as they nodded and smiled at her. "Can you tell us now who you are?"

The girl's eyes, still indicating a feeling of apprehension, inspected them, then dejectedly turned away shaking her head. "I . . . I'm sorry. I can't seem to remember anything."

"Do you remember trying to steal our horse last night?" Joel questioned.

"Steal a horse?" Her, dark, brown eyes grew huge, "Oh, no . . . oh . . . yes. Yes, I do remember that."

"Would you care to explain? You know horse stealing is a mighty serious offense. A horse in the west is practically a man's life."

The petite form lay very still for a long moment. Then she

looked with such innocence, a countenance so forlorn, so pitiful at the five figures standing around her bed.

"Surely this lovely lady couldn't do any real harm to anyone, not intentionally anyway. She must have been desperate."
Joel's thoughts began to soften.

Words finally came. "I can't remember why, but I remember running. I don't know where I was going, or from whom.
All I know is . . . I . . . I just had to get away. I must have been
running off and on for days. I can remember finding some
clothes in an old deserted shack up in the mountains. My dress
had been torn to shreds, and I was so very tired and hungry. I
found some stale bread and dried pieces of meat in the cabin.
Nothing ever tasted so good to me in my whole life . . . except
the broth that Sarah brought me." She directed her eyes toward Sarah and presented an appreciative smile. "I wanted to
lie down and sleep so badly, but I knew I couldn't stay there
because they would find me." Her voice became full of distress. A tear slid down her cheek.

"They? Who are 'they'?" Mark interrupted her.

"I . . . umm . . . I don't know. Three men. I can remember
three men were chasing me. I knew they would hurt me. I had
to run." She broke off sobbing.

"There, there, honey. No one is going to hurt you now,"
Joel said very calmly. His heart reached out to her. "We'll see
to that. Do you recall anything about these men?"

Her tear-stained face looked up to his, "No, sir. I just
knew they would hurt me, and I had to keep running before
they found me."

"Well, we've tired you enough for one day. You lie back
down now, and get some more rest. We'll talk again in the
morning. If you need us for anything, you call. Sarah, here,
will stay with you." He looked at Sarah and she shook her
head, yes.

The four men left the room. Watery eyes filled with anguish followed them. She turned to Sarah who smiled tenderly. The girl returned her smile. At last she breathed a sigh of relief. Her frightened expression disappeared from those dark brown eyes, which gradually closed, falling into a restless sleep.

The men had reclined on comfortable chairs around the large, stone fireplace in the living room. "What do you think, Pa? Was she telling the truth?" Tom asked.

"I prefer to think she was, Tom. Apparently she has a reason for being frightened. I'd sure like to get a hold of those three despicable creatures that call themselves men. I'd sure find out why they've scared her so."

"I noticed she was wearing a gold wedding band," remarked Paul.

"Yes. I saw it, too," the father replied.

"Do you suppose one of these men could have been her husband?"

"I don't know, Mark. Could be, but it doesn't sound much like it to me."

The men sat in quiet, while pondering over their individual thoughts for a while. After a time Sarah came out of the bedroom, informed them the girl had fallen asleep, and asked if she would be needed. If not, she would like to retire herself. It had been a busy day for all, and she felt very tired.

Joel thanked her and said she had been a great help to them, to go onto bed and get some well-deserved rest.

The three sons withdrew to their own rooms, while their father situated his weary body in his impressive overstuffed chair for a few minutes to relax. Peacefulness spread through the large log house. He sat peering into the flickering flames, listening to the crackling of the wood in the beautifully crafted stone fireplace he had built many years ago with the help of his friend, Luke Judson. Now, it fell his lot to face another circumstance without his beloved wife with which to share his thoughts. But Mattie had given him three fine sons, young men now. With his steadfast faith in God, and his sons who provided him so much stability, he would carry on just fine. For through experience he had learned the God that comforts our saddened hearts, also gladdens our weary souls.

Joel McCalister's tall frame and ruggedly attractive features showed only touches of silver threads mingling in his sideburns. A man in his early fifties, he had broad shoulders, strong muscular arms, and an aura about him that made one accept this man as one of authority. Always known for his fairness and honesty in his words and actions, he also had a remarkable sense of humor, which won him many friends.

Joel's surrounding neighbors and friends regarded him as a man of wisdom. Often they came to him for advice in innumerable occasions, because they knew Joel McCalister would be honest with them in a compassionate way. Many admired him for his courage; a few despised him because they were jealous to see such strength and wisdom in another man. A man who would stand up to their kind, to fight for what was right if need be. Still, Joel did not fight unless needlessly provoked; he knew there were times when it takes a bigger man to step away from a feud, than to strike out in anger. But when a human life was at stake, a person was being abused, threatened, Joel didn't hesitate to step in. "Right's right, and we must stand up for that which is right," he often reasoned.

He enjoyed discussing the Bible or the changing world with some people, the subject of statehood with others. Now statehood, *that* subject he relished. In the twenty-five years Joel and Mattie resided in the west, they had witnessed many changes. Not long after settling on their land, the people north of the Columbia River decided it would be more profitable to separate from the Territory of Oregon and form their own territory. The name, Territory of Columbia, had been decided upon, but changed to "Washington" in honor of the first president of the United States, when brought before Congress. To see this territory he and his sons help colonize become one of the United States of America excited the next hope and dream for the McCalisters and their neighbors. Yet, convincing some in Congress didn't provide an easy task.

Yes, the pristine west was a new challenge Mattie and Joel had shared together. But, now the body of his precious Mattie lay resting under the large maple tree she had planted many years ago. Mattie, the one who always shared his dreams before would not be here to see Washington become a state. Her sons would, he felt convinced, and that allowed a consolation to Joel. He certainly would miss his beloved Mattie. Yes, he already did. However, through their sons—their seeds of love—the tomorrows were still worth living. The trials of life may mount ahead, and there would surely be some, but they would be faced with divine guidance through prayer to the Heavenly Father above.

"Man, I'd sure like to get my hands on those three no good mavericks who would so unmercifully frighten a young woman into becoming a fugitive on the run," Joel thought out loud with disgust in his voice, pounding his fist in his hand.

The fire in the fireplace had turned into embers; Joel didn't realize how long he had been meditating. He decided he'd better retire to his lonely bed. Tomorrow was another day. Morning comes early to a rancher; to some folks a half a day's work would be accomplished before the breakfast meal. Maybe the distraught girl could remember more after she had rested another night. He surely hoped so.

Dr. Rider knocked at the door of the McCalister home the next afternoon. "Come in. Come in, Doc. We're mighty glad to see you," greeted Joel, his hand outstretched. "We didn't know you were back from your trip already. What do we owe this unexpected pleasure to . . . fate or good luck?"

"Well, now, Joel, I thank you for those nice considerate words, but I happened to see Mrs. Judson in town this morning. She told me something about you folks finding a sick girl in your corral, or somewhere. So I decided I'd better come on out here and see if I could be of some service."

Joel went over the account of how the girl chanced to be with them, and that she was unable to give them any information as to whom she is or where she's from.

"Let's have a look at this little lady. You say she's slept most of the time? Well, sleep never hurt anyone. It certainly sounds like she needed rest," remarked the doctor.

Sarah was sitting by the girl's bed in a rocking chair, when they entered the room. She had been telling her about the Judson family. The petite figure was sitting up in bed smiling. They both said hello to Joel, but when the girl noticed the stranger enter, a frightened expression returned to her face.

"Young lady, I'd like to introduce you to Dr. Rider. He would like to check you over to see if he can find anything wrong with you," smiled Joel. "He's been a friend of the family for years, so we all know he wouldn't harm a flea."

"That's certainly right there, Miss. All my friends tell me my dog has the most fleas in town," chuckled the doctor.

The girl managed a smile, as the rest gave way to laughter. Joel motioned to Sarah for them to leave the room. Time seemed to pass by very slowly after they left. Nearly an hour later the doctor came out. He accepted the cup of coffee offered him, then spoke, "Seems to me, Joel, there doesn't appear to be much wrong with your guest physically. She is undernourished, and needs to be built up with good healthy food, which I know she'll get here. She is pretty delicate, but I don't see why tomorrow she can't start getting out of bed and moving around again. Just a few minutes at a time at first, gradually increasing her stamina. By the end of the week her full strength should be restored."

"That sounds very encouraging, Doc."

"Yes, Joel, it's encouraging to know that she's well physically. I'm sorry to say there's another problem. She has all the symptoms of amnesia. Her type of amnesia is apparently caused by a severe shock. It is evident she has been unable to cope with, or accept some painful experience in her life. To an amnesia victim, the only solution is to deny who she is or where she's from. When this emotional conflict is resolved, her memory should begin to return. Sometimes this is a very slow process. She may do things that might remind her of the past. Or possibly the experience may return very sudden, or maybe worse, not at all. It's something we can't know. Right now you folks are the only family she has. She'll depend on you a great deal. Gradually she should get out and meet more people and rejoin the world again. That may not be easy for her."

"Hmm, apparently I am now a father of three sons and a daughter! Thank you, Doc, for coming out here. And as long as you're in our home, you may as well stay for supper."

"That sounds like a fine idea. I accept the invitation," he grinned at his friend.

The young visitor joined the McCalister family the following morning while they were seated for breakfast. Her appearance was most welcome, and she looked lovely in the borrowed pink robe belonging to Sarah. Her long auburn hair was caught in the back by a satin ribbon. Her large, dark brown eyes had a sparkle to them. A faint splash of pink color started to become visible in her pale cheeks. Each of the men rose to offer her a chair; she accepted the one next to Mark, the closest.

"Good morning," she spoke amiably, smiling to each one

a little shyly. "The doctor told me yesterday that I should start getting up and about, so I decided I would like to join you for breakfast."

Sarah brought another table setting, as Mark helped her with her chair.

"We're glad to have you join with us," announced Joel. "Say, young lady, there's been one thing running through my mind this morning. Since you have this here thing called amnesia, and can't recall your name, what shall we call you? We can't go around addressing you, 'Hey, girl,' all the time."

They all laughed, then the young woman said demurely, "I guess you're right. I'm going to need a name . . . any suggestions?"

"How about Bessie?"

"Naw. We have a cow named Bessie and she's the meanest of them all," Sarah teased.

"Clementine?"

"Ah, no."

"Sally?"

"How about Julie? Wasn't that Grandmother McCalister's name?" suggested Paul.

"Julie. Very pretty. I like that," the girl consented, nodding her head in agreement.

"Fine, then. We've settled it. We'll call you Julie," said Mr. McCalister. "Now that we have solved that minor problem, let's eat. I'm starved!"

They all agreed unanimously, as Sarah brought in a large stack of hotcakes, sausages, and eggs filling the room with the delicious aroma.

Two

Friendship, what a precious gift. Most persons come in contact with many people during a lifetime. Some are merely acquaintances, some become friends, and many depart and are soon placed in the background of our minds. It has been said that friends are like tears—as tears fall, some crystallize into diamonds and remain precious and rare; some are like autumn leaves, drifting everywhere. Friends, true friends, are a blessing from God; they, too, are precious and rare. Three weeks have drifted by since Mattie's death and Julie has come to be a part of the McCalister family. Three insignificant weeks and yet a blooming friendship began to flourish between Julie and Sarah. These two young women knew in their hearts the friendship they shared would always remain true, precious and rare.

Sarah had returned to her family, when they all felt Julie was strong enough to help with household duties. Sarah promised to visit the McCalister ranch as often as she could to help out, if needed. The days were turning back into a normal life for the McCalister men. Julie had insisted she take over the duties of the house, as long as she lived there with her new family. She didn't want to be a burden on them, wanting to be useful in any way possible, and felt very glad to be feeling strong and able once again.

Straightening up and cleaning the huge log house became a delight for Julie. Mattie had evidently trained her men well, since she found most of their belongings put in their proper places. Dusting the furniture, tidying up the beds, and cleaning the floors became a routine; although washing the clothes of four men, drying them on the back porch when it was raining, and pressing them with an iron, which needed to be heated on the stove, didn't become her favorite chore. A necessary task, nevertheless, to be done at least weekly, she accepted without complaining, at least to the men. However, she did allow some complaining to herself once in a while instead.

Now cooking, that was something else. She seemed to have some ideas on the subject; but she soon established she wasn't very accomplished at the task of planning meals and preparing the foods. A good-sized stove and plenty of pots and pans were plentiful. Why the foods she cooked turned out either burned or half done, her reasoning couldn't quite figure out. She wanted so earnestly to please the men. They were very patient, even though they teased her at times. Still, she knew she needed some help, especially after last evening's disaster.

Yesterday morning she had found a ham hock one of the men had brought in from the storehouse and placed on the table. With it she decided to fix a pot of beans for the main meal. Not knowing how much salt to put in the pot, she concluded, a fourth of a cup would surely be plenty. It was . . . along with a fourth of a cup of pepper. When the men dished up the beans that evening at suppertime, they knew something was wrong when the beans rattled loudly on their plates. Being the kind gentlemen that they were, as well as starved, one by one each took a bite, and one by one they asked to be excused from the table, while holding their hands over their mouths. When Julie tasted her bite, she regretfully understood why they weren't staying to finish the meal.

The next day Sarah happened to come by. Julie was in the process of throwing out another one of her culinary calamities to the few chickens, who squawked at her as if to say, "Oh, no! We're not eating another mess again today!"

"Hi, Julie, whatcha got there?"

"Oh, Sarah, I'm just not a cook. When I fry eggs, the bacon is burned. When I cook pancakes, they're either not done in the center or they turnout blackened. I could go on and on. I try so hard, still nothing ever comes out right." Her face looked so forlorn.

"Okay. I've learned a lot from Mama. Let me help you prepare something for today."

"Thank you. If you're sure you have the time." Julie sighed heavily.

First they gleaned a few vegetables from the garden close by, and discovered some jars of canned goods in the storehouse not far from the back porch. Soon they were busy peeling potatoes, carrots and added all varieties of vegetables in a large pot. It wasn't long until the house filled with the succulent aroma of stew. Some apples had also been found in the storehouse, so Sarah set out to teach her friend how to make applesauce and pie crust for several apple pies.

When the men sat down at the dinner table that evening with wonder on their faces—wondering if they had anything edible to eat for a change—they didn't know that Sarah had visited that day. Julie set the table with a bowl of fresh, warm applesauce and golden brown biscuits, and then dished up the stew to each individual man.

"Umm, sure smells good," Joel said trying to sound pleased, still wondering what the taste might be. As he took a small bite, all eyes were on him. He grinned. "Say! This is really good! You've outdone yourself today, little lady."

With a big sigh, Julie thanked him, and everyone else began to eat. The biscuits were a little hard, but edible, the pie a masterpiece. Of course Sarah was the one who made the crust. Still, Julie had sliced the apples, and with her friend's instructions added the sugar, butter and spices. She finally felt pleased and anxious for another lesson from her endearing confidant the following day. Sarah had offered to give her some lessons on the art of cooking until Julie felt confident she could handle the chore.

Dear, blessed Sarah became a lifesaver to not only Julie, but to the stomachs of the McCalister men. Each day they tried something different: a roast with potatoes and carrots; a meat loaf with baked potatoes, a variety of pies and cookies, and so on. The men were amazed at the change in Julie's talents, until she finally admitted her friend had shared some recipes and volunteered to give her some instructions in cooking.

Cooking became an enjoyment to the young woman now. Just seeing the gratifying expressions on the men's faces stirred her encouragement. A gourmet cook she was not, however, the desire challenged her to be at least a sufficient one.

An announcement at the supper table one evening stated that next Saturday night the Hawleys were giving a party; a special event, because the Hawleys would be celebrating their fiftieth wedding anniversary. Seth Hawley commented jovially many times to his friends, "If a man had the fortitude to stay married to the same woman for fifty l-l-o-o-n-n-g-g years, then the world should know about it!" After Saturday night, at least this minute part of the sparsely populated Pacific Northwest would be enlightened. People had been invited for miles around the area.

It took the McCalisters and Sarah a lot of talking to convince Julie that she should attend the festivities, meet more people, and get back into trusting the world again. At last persuaded, the four men sat around the comfortable living room discussing the momentous event to take place, while Julie carried out the finishing touches of cleaning the kitchen area.

"You know, Pa," commented Paul, "I've been giving it some thought. Since we've persuaded Julie into going to this

get-together, I think we should present her with a gift of elo-
quence."

"Like what, son?"

"I was thinking maybe we should buy Julie one of those
store-bought dresses. You know, she doesn't have a dress of
her own. Sarah has been kind enough to share some of her
clothes, but she should have something of her own to wear, especially to the celebration."

"That's a swell idea," agreed Tom.

"I've gotta go in to town on business tomorrow. I'll take
her with me and she can pick out a dress then," confirmed
Joel.

"Why don't we surprise her?" suggested Mark.

"Good idea," proclaimed the men in unison.

After a minute or two the father countered, "Who's going
to do the buying?"

"How about you, Pa? You know more about women than
us," spoke up Mark. "And you said you have to go in to town
anyway."

"Uh, ah . . . my business will take too long. Why not you,
Paul? You made the suggestion," stammered Joel.

"Another great idea," Tom hurriedly added, pleased his
name wasn't mentioned.

"Hey, wait a minute! I don't know anything about buying
a dress!" responded Paul, grimacing.

"Now is as good a time as any to learn," chuckled one of
the other men.

"Well, well. What's all the laughing about in here? Have I
been missing out on something?" Julie entered the room with
a smile on her face.

"Oh, Paul here just told us one of his old yarns. We just
laughed to be polite," Tom answered, giving Paul a wink.

The men and Julie all glanced at Paul's scarlet face, then
they all started to laugh.

Paul was hoping tomorrow would never come. But it did, bright and early. Joel had the buckboard all ready to go, when the two brothers pushed Paul out the door. "We might as well get some needed supplies while we're in town." Joel handed his son a list. Julie ran outside with a list of her own.

The five miles into Cascadia seemed exceedingly short to Paul, when they pulled up to the general store. "Pa, are you sure you wouldn't like to purchase the dress?" He looked at his father pleadingly.

"You'll do all right, son. Just tell Mrs. Jones what you want. She'll help you." With that, Joel hurried away, leaving Paul standing there feeling very much alone.

Finally, he entered the well-stocked store. He looked around a few minutes, then ordered the supplies.

"Will this be all I can do for you?" asked the cheerful Mrs. Jones.

"Huh, a . . . well, no ma . . . ma'am," stammered Paul. "I'd like . . . to buy . . . a . . . dress."

The woman glanced at him somewhat startled.

"Oh . . . ah . . . it's not for me!" Paul quickly added, appearing miserably flustered. "It's for a girl. You know, the girl that's staying with us for a while."

"Well, I assumed it wasn't for you," chuckled the woman with a big grin. "Yes, I've heard about her. Let's see, her name is Julie, isn't it?" Paul nodded a yes. "Okay. Now what size would she wear?" Mrs. Jones asked.

"Size? Golly, ma'am, I don't know. She's about so high and . . . " Paul tried measuring with his hands.

"Is she about my size?" questioned the tall, very thin woman.

"No, ma'am. She's . . . ah . . . more like . . . ah . . . Sarah Judson."

"Fine. Is this for the anniversary celebration?" Again,

Paul nodded a yes. "I think I just might have a suitable dress. Came in just recently. Come over here," motioned the woman.

An hour later the men rejoined each other at the buckboard. "How did the venture go?" inquired the father, sporting a broad smile and a twinkle in his eyes.

"All right, I guess. But Pa, don't ever suggest I do that again!" With that settled, Joel patted his son on the shoulder and set their sights for home.

Following the evening meal, Julie was escorted to the sofa in the cozy living room, then Joel presented her with a huge, elegantly wrapped package decorated with a silk bow.

"Julie, this is for you because we all think so much of you," Joel spoke with a genuine sincerity in his voice.

She looked surprised, and then with excitement tore open the gift. First she found a pair of shoes: black patented leather, high stepped with a row of buttons . . . the latest style Mrs. Jones had assured Paul. Julie glanced at each of the men appreciatively, and started to speak . . .

"Go on, there's something else," encouraged Paul.

Then she removed a layer of tissue paper. There it was, a delicate mint green dress. Julie slowly lifted the lovely fashion out of the large box, and held it to her bosom. It was exquisite and feminine, with a rounded neckline, a full ruffled skirt and lots of dainty lace.

"Oh . . . it's so elegant." Julie couldn't believe her eyes. "Is it really for me? My very own dress?"

"I don't think any of us would look good in it," teased Tom.

"Yes, Julie, the dress is a gift especially for you," the father proudly replied.

"Thank you. Thank you all so very much," was all Julie could say over and over again. "It's just beautiful!" and the tears began to flow. "How can I ever repay you for all that you've done for me?"

"Aw shucks, ma'am," Tom said. "We all love you." With that the four men, in turns, whirled her around the room. A satisfying way to end a perfect evening in the McCalister homestead.

After Julie departed to her room, Paul said, "She really liked it, didn't she?"

"It's been a long time since I've seen anyone so happy around here. It kinda gives a person a worthwhile feeling. Say, what a smart idea about the shoes," commented Mark.

"That was Mrs. Jones' idea. She said a new dress deserved some new shoes."

"Just like a woman," uttered Joel, as he laughed. "Well, this has been an edifying day. Let's get to bed. I'm tired."

Saturday night finally arrived. The men sat around talking about the day's encounters, while waiting for Julie. Ultimately, she came out of her room. Mark noticed her first, rising slowly, speechless.

"Julie, you're magnificent, simply beautiful!" exclaimed Joel. The other three added their approvals.

Julie glowed radiantly as she twirled around showing off her gorgeous new dress. It fit perfectly . . . although the shoes had to be exchanged for a smaller pair. Her glistening auburn hair was fashioned into curls on top of her head with three ringlets cascading down to one side. All afternoon she had been consumed in preparing for the social gathering. She wanted everyone to be proud of her, as she was of them. The time labored in preparation appeared well worth the effort. The expression of approval on the men's faces confirmed that to her, making her happy, gloriously happy.

"Shall we go?" The father stood up.

"Let's get going." The agreement sounded as they set out

in the direction of the Hawleys' celebration. A warm spring night with a brilliant full moon and shimmering stars brightened the evening sky. A fragrance of lilacs and honeysuckle filled the air. Laughter and singing abounded from the buckboard, while they rode the four miles to their neighbor's ranch. What a special night. This was also Julie's "Coming Out Party."

Carriages and buckboards by the dozens occupied much of the area around the Hawleys' rustic barn. A barn became the natural place for a get-together in the west. Ranchers and farmers could spare little time for parties. Usually, when someone puts on a shindig, everyone in the area receives and invitation. Sons, daughters, grandchildren, neighbors all helped decorate the large barn for this special occasion. Strings of kerosene lanterns lined the short path to the austere building. One could hardly imagine a few hours earlier it housed cattle and horses. Even the barnyard aroma was faint, everyone was used to that anyway, so what little there was went unnoticed and forgiven.

Each one who thought he could play an instrument brought one. Music became an important element in the social life of the early pioneers. Tom had brought along his mouth organ, and joined the musical section consisting of banjos, fiddles, guitars, accordions, and even one of the families had transported their prized piano in the back of their wagon for this grand occasion. A snowy-haired gentleman with a long white beard could be heard calling out a square dance. The building was already half full with more arriving intermittently.

Soon after the McCalisters and Julie entered the building, a middle-aged woman came over to greet them. "You must be Julie," she smiled at the girl. "I'm Emma Judson. Sarah has talked a great deal about you. We're so glad you came tonight, and I'm so pleased I finally have the opportunity to meet you."

Mrs. Judson was an attractive woman of average height, slightly overweight, but a pleasing figure for a mother of ten. Laugh lines showed around her hazel eyes and full mouth. Julie liked her instantly.

Just then Sarah glanced their way and strolled over. She was captivating in her dress of soft blue, matching her eyes. Her shiny blond hair, tied underneath by a velvet blue ribbon, fell in deep waves down her shoulders. "Hi Julie," she greeted her new friend. "I'm so glad you decided to come. I see you've met my mother."

"Sarah, you look absolutely stunning. Is this the dress you fashioned yourself?" asked Julie.

"Uh-huh. Yours is so pretty. I hope you like it. I heard about Paul picking it out." She grinned. "Come on. I want you to meet some of my other friends. They're anxious to meet you. Excuse us, Mama?"

"Of course, dear," answered Mrs. Judson, smiling as she turned to Joel. "She's a delightful girl, Joel. She must be a great help to you since Mattie's death."

"Yes, she certainly has been, Emma. Julie's the daughter Mattie and I never had. How's Luke? I see he brought his fiddle along."

"You know Luke Judson. He wouldn't be seen at a get-together without his fiddle," with that they chuckled and strolled over to greet some more friends. Joel glanced around the room, focusing on Julie and Sarah talking to a group of young people. Paul and Mark had joined them.

"Come on, Julie, let's join the line for the 'Virginia Reel,'" Paul coaxed her. "Just follow me, it's easy."

"I'll try, if Sarah and Mark will join us."

"Sure," Mark agreed, then looking at Sarah, he asked, "Okay, lovely lady?"

There was no doubt in Julie's mind. Mark indeed proved to be one of the handsomest men in the crowd. His dark, curly hair and bright, blue eyes sparkled when he laughed. Deep dimples formed in his cheeks from his laughter, making him appear much younger than his twenty-one years. His voice and mannerisms were all masculine, along with his muscular six-foot frame. Julie almost envied her friend.

A waltz changed the tempo from the square dance. "Oh, that was fun, but this is more my style," Julie admitted.

"You did fine," Paul assured his partner. After a pause, "You look exceptionally beautiful tonight, Julie. Are you enjoying yourself?"

"It's been grand, Paul. As you know, I felt somewhat apprehensive about coming. But your friends are very kind. They've gone out of their way to be nice and make me feel welcome." She gazed in his blue-gray eyes. "Sarah informed me that you picked out my dress. I truly hope you know how proud I am. I'm sure it's the prettiest gown I've ever had."

"Let's walk outside so we can talk." Paul smiled, somewhat embarrassed.

"All right. It is getting a little stuffy in here."

They managed their way to the back door of the barn and on out past the corral. The cool breeze felt refreshing. A fragrance of roses and early summer flowers filled the evening air. The moonlit night made it easy for them to pick out a pathway. They sauntered up to the crest of a nearby grassy knoll before speaking a word. Julie was the one to break the silence.

"This is such magnificent country, Paul. The evergreens stand so straight. The rolling hills and green valleys with rugged rivers and streams flowing in and out weave an intricate scene for an artist's dreamland. I often wonder if I am from around here. I do so wish I knew. It's so lovely and yet I'm not all together comfortable with this area. Truly God's love for beauty is displayed in this part of His world."

"I hope we can help you remember your past. It must be

difficult not knowing who you are, or where you're from, and where your family might be. We have grown up taking pride in our land. My father and mother settled here nearly twenty-five years ago. Mark and I were born on the ranch, Tom back East. Pa really worked hard for what we have. He logged the trees to build their first cabin, then several years later the Indians set fire to it in a raid. We lost everything. I can remember my brothers and I helping Pa build the house we now live in. We were pretty small, but felt mighty important just the same. Our neighbors all came over to help. The Judsons and Mr. and Mrs. Hawley were the first ones to come to our rescue. These dear friends brought food, clothes, and even a few pieces of furniture crafted by Mr. Hawley himself. They really couldn't afford it, but that's the kind of people we have here. When a family has troubles, or joys, we all share them together."

"Just like you, your Pa, and your brothers have shown me. I try to steal a horse, and instead of condemning me, you take me in and let me share your home. I don't know how I'll ever repay you and your family for your kindness."

"Isn't that really what people are for, Julie? To help one another, to love one another?" He then looked at his lovely companion with moonlight sparkling in her dark brown eyes. A red tint to her hair shimmered, as if it were afire. The curve of her mouth, her soft fair skin; how captivating she was. How he yearned to hold her in his arms. But, she wore a band of gold on her third finger left hand. She belonged to someone else. "I, I'd better get you back to the party before they start missing us, and come looking."

"Yes, I guess we'd better." Except Julie really didn't want to lose this priceless moment. Paul was the easygoing, gentle man of the family with his charming smile, blue-gray eyes, ruddy complexion and dark wavy hair. He always seemed to have an acute sense of making one feel at ease, as Julie felt now. Then she touched her ring and wondered if she belonged to someone else. She tried to hide the sigh of despair, as she gave him a shy smile.

He helped her to her feet, and they slowly walked back toward the gaily decorated barn. As they approached the building, sounds of laughter mixed with music filled the air. Suddenly the music stopped, and the crowd grew silent. A middle-aged man was attracting the attention of the audience, while claiming his place on the platform where the caller with the long white beard had stood before.

"Ladies and gentlemen," he began, as the crowd quieted down while Julie and Paul wedged their way into the building. "Tonight we are here to honor a fine couple who have been a part of our lives. We could go on through the night reminiscing on all the kind deeds these dear people here bestowed upon us, but I'll share only one.

"Most of you will remember the day our little son fell in the well back of our house. Seth Hawley risked his life to rescue our James. Seth insisted I lower him down into that cold, dark well, then he tied the rope onto our son, and helped hoist him up out of danger. All the while, Seth here, patiently waited in the chilling water for the rope to be thrown back so I could retrieve him. My grateful heart will always be thankful for this man of steadfast courage. And to his dear wife, Molly, who has been a midwife for many of our spouses through the years. The rest of you, I know, have equally rich memories you could share, but we'll let them remain in our hearts at this time, because they number too many to mention this evening.

"Now, on behalf of everyone in our midst, I have been given the honor and privilege of presenting to the Hawleys this small token of our appreciation for the years of friendship and kind deeds they have shown to us all."

The elderly couple stood beside the speaker, their eyes beaming. Both were very thin, slight in stature, yet appeared healthy enough to enjoy their seventy-fifth anniversary when the time comes.

"Well, bless my soul! Look here what we got, Papa. Why folks, I'm just dumbfounded. Thank you, ever'body. Thank you." Tears started to stream down the little lady's face, as she admired the solid gold coffee service: pitcher, creamer, sugar bowl and tray, imported from the old country from which they originally came.

"Come on, Seth and Molly, you must lead the grand waltz," encouraged the man who had made the presentation.

The musicians began to play as the honored couple flowed with the music. "My, my, Papa, we'll have to do this more often!" exclaimed Molly, and everyone who heard were once again amused, joining the beloved couple on the hard earthen floor.

All too swiftly the evening passed by and guests needed to head towards home. Morning would come bright and early, and there were always chores to perform before the morning service would begin in the humble community church in town. As little work as possible was performed on the Lord's Day, but certain things had to be attended to.

Everyone had a splendid time. No one in the McCalister family desired to break the spell of enchantment the evening had woven in their memories during the silent ride back to the ranch.

Three

On the afternoon following the memorable celebration, the brothers decided the time was right for Julie to get on the back of a horse so she would be able to go shopping, visiting, or whatever, as Tom stated it. With a lot of protest from the girl, and more encouragement from the men, a sorrel mare was saddled.

"Have you ever ridden a horse before, Julie?" Mark asked.

"I don't know. But these butterflies I have fluttering in my stomach tell me it's not the most natural thing I've ever done," she replied.

"Well, let's see if you can mount the mare," urged Tom. "Don't be frightened. Her name is Scarlet. I picked her especially for you, because her hair matches yours, and she's the gentlest horse on the ranch."

Julie timidly walked toward the corral. The horse of choice seemed to magnify in size, as she trudged ever so slowly towards the animal. Not wanting to appear too wimpy, and before the men could say a word, she attempted to climb on its back from the right side. The horse bucked away, causing Julie to fall on rocky ground. Joel came out of the house just at that moment and noticed the girl sitting with her face cupped in her hands and elbows propped up on her legs. Her disheveled hair had fallen down over her eyes, and the bewildered expression on her face proved comical.

"What happened here?" he asked.

She couldn't help but notice a slight grin on his face. "Well, sir, his head went down and his tail went up, and he stepped all over me with his claws!" Julie exclaimed. The four men burst with laughter. Julie couldn't see anything humorous about the frightful incident, while attempting to get up.

"Are you hurt?" Paul asked with concern, but trying to hide a smile. He reached over to offer his hand.

"Nope. Just hurt my seat a little." She started rubbing her backside. They roared with more laughter. Julie couldn't understand what would cause them to behave in such a manner. "Why, I might have been killed!" she thought out loud. "The nerve of these big bruisers, standing there making fun of me." It was too much. Her pride being hurt, off she stormed to the ranch house, slamming the door upon entering.

By the end of the following week, Julie found riding the sorrel less troublesome. The men had finally convinced her that even the best horsemen have fallen from a horse at one time or another, even if they saddled the animal on the correct side. It's easier and quicker to get into a saddle on the left side, they had explained. Now with insistent determination Julie desired to master the art of at least, "Staying on the back of the beast without being bumped off."

Paul decided to take her for a ride . . . outside of the corral. After riding a mile or more along a stony trail through the dense forest, Julie began to tire, her legs stiff and sore from the previous lessons. "How about we stop somewhere and walk a while?" She looked over at Paul with pleading eyes.

"Sure, Julie. We can head over to that clump of trees at the base of the hill. Let's go for a hike. There's something I'd like you to see at the crest of the hill. Maybe a little walking will loosen you up a bit."

"Sounds like a good idea," she agreed, anything to get off that four-legged animal.

34

Paul tied the horses to a stately fir, while Julie stretched her legs and rubbed her calves as well as other aching places.

"You ready to start?"

"Sure."

The rocky path wound its way upward through a heavily wooded forest of Douglas fir, tamarack, cedar and numerous evergreens. Some of the trees were so huge it would have taken several men grasping hands to reach around their circumference.

"Oh, look, Paul, a chipmunk!" Julie exclaimed. "How adorable." The curious reddish-brown animal with two black stripes running down its tail scampered away, when she reached out her hand to the tiny rodent. Every once in a while they would find a colorful wild flower mixed in among the ferns, moss and underbrush. Paul knelt to pick a dainty white lily, which he stuck in her hair. A faint sound of a waterfall could be heard in the distance.

"Can we get close enough to see the waterfall?"

"Why sure. Take my hand. It's pretty rough, but it's worth the trek."

Julie fell over a log, and had to be helped up, then tripped over some more low-lying branches. When they finally reached the edge of a clearing, there in full view nature's magnificence displayed the powerful splendor of cascading water.

"It's absolutely breathtaking. Look! There's a fawn and its mother," she called out excitedly. "Ohh, he ran away."

Although not a large one, twenty feet or so, the waterfall seemed to release tons of mountain fresh water spilling over the jagged boulders, causing a roaring sound as it splashed on the rocks below. On further the gushing creek produced another, smaller cascade of water tumbling over rugged rocks. The two rested on the bank for a few moments in silence, letting the rest of the world flow by, while watching and listening to the sounds of nature's beauty.

Finally Paul broke the enchanted spell. "Shall we go? I still have something else I want you to see."

"All right," Julie smiled dreamily.

As soon as they ascended the craggy trail, she noticed more busy chipmunks joined by light gray squirrels with red bushy tails chattering as if miffed because they were being intruded by unwelcome strangers. Finally, they ran off hiding amongst multi-hued wild flowers. The air smelled fresh and invigorating. A glorious view from the crown of the hill overlooked a peaceful picturesque valley centered by a small green lake which reflected stately firs, pines, and snow-capped mountains. Indeed our Creator formed a resplendent scene untouched by human hands in a world all its own.

"Thank you, Paul, for allowing me to come and share with you such a superb, secret place. I've never seen anything more lovely. This has been an awesome day for me. I never realized life could be so exciting, full of adventure. And the lake . . . it reminds me of the green emerald my mother always wore."

"Your mother?" Paul captured her words instantly. "What else do you recall about your mother?"

"Wha . . . what? I, I don't know! I just . . . remember . . . a green emerald." A wrinkle shown in her forehead. "I just remember she wore a green emerald necklace around her neck."

After a moment, "Anything else? Can you picture her face?"

"No." She placed her hands on either side of her face, then releasing a sigh, "No. I'm sorry, Paul."

"Well, maybe this is a start. We'll have to come back here again. Let's call this Emerald Lake, okay?" Paul spoke gently, giving her a concerned smile.

"Perfect."

"Hey, there's a fish. See it flip up in the water? I'm going to catch it." Paul found a long, narrow branch, took his knife and sharpened the end of the stick. "If Indians can harpoon a fish, maybe I can." A mischievous grin lit up his face, then he galloped down the hillside.

His luck wasn't at all profitable the first few tries. Not one to give up, and nearly an hour of falling in the water, while being good-naturedly teased by his female companion, Paul made a catch. One to be proud of? Umm, not exactly. In fact, any seasoned fisherman would have thrown the fish back, but nope. He had worked too hard for this slippery catch.

Julie sat on the lake's edge laughing, as Paul, drenching wet, came trudging out of the water proudly displaying his miniature prize impaled to the stick. "Ha, ha. That was more fun than falling off a horse's back," she continued with playful ridicule.

"So you think I'm funny, eh?" grinned Paul, as he picked her up, the petite figure kicking and screaming, as he carried her toward the lake. "Don't you dare!" Still, he tossed her in the water anyway.

Julie finally managed to sit up in the icy water. "Oh, you beast!" She cried out. Then she began to laugh again, while wading to shore. Her dripping outfit clung to her slender frame.

"I reckon we'd better head back to the ranch before we both catch our death of cold," Paul managed to say through his snickering. He picked up his fishing "gear," took Julie by the hand and off they went.

However, they hadn't gone far when it started to sprinkle. Soon the drops turned into a downpour. "I know where there's an old deserted trapper's shack just over that ridge. We could stay there till the rain stops. Maybe we can start up a warm fire."

"And cook the fish?" Julie couldn't help but add a little

teasing. Then said, "It does sound great," as a shiver ran through her body.

Back at the ranch the other three men were getting restless. "Surely they should be back by now, Pa. Do you suppose something is wrong?" Mark showed concern.

"Paul can take care of himself, son." But the brothers could see the anguished look in their father's eyes. Paul and Julie had been gone several hours. There could be something amiss. Julie usually had supper cooking by now.

"I think I'll just scout around," remarked Tom, always the protective one. "I'm sure they are all right, but they will be soaking wet. The rain is really coming down hard. I'll take some dry blankets in my pack and see if I might run into them."

"Good idea, son. Be careful. We don't want to have to hunt for you, too."

By the time Tom saddled his horse the rain had slowed down to a drizzle, gradually stopping, for which he was pleased. The horse's tracks had been washed away by the unsympathetic shower. But he had noticed the general direction which the two chose earlier that morning.

It didn't take him long to find two agitated horses tied to a tree. Tom knew the area well. "They must have found shelter in that old abandoned cabin," he surmised to himself. At least he hoped so. He made his way on horseback until he noticed the run-down shack, then tied his horse to a tree and went the few yards on foot.

The door to the dwelling was open. As he drew closer, he noticed fresh hoof prints made by several horses around the cabin door. Hurrying inside, he heard moaning, and found Paul lying on the floor. Paul tried to get up when he heard Tom enter, only to fall back down. His head was covered with blood.

"Paul! Paul! What happened?" Tom burst out. "Where's Julie?"

"Julie! Oh, no! They've taken Julie! Tom, we've got to go after them. They'll kill her."

"Who are they? Who took Julie?"

"Indians," then Paul went on to relate his story. As he and Julie were nearing the shack, someone came up behind them. He heard Julie scream, then saw the face of an Indian. That's all he could remember till he came to, just as Tom approached the cabin.

"They must have thought they had killed me, so they dragged my body in here. Probably would have set fire to the cabin, but heard you coming and took off . . . with Julie!"

"We'd better get you back to the ranch first, and get Pa and Mark. You're lucky they didn't scalp you. Their trail should be easy enough to pick up in this mud."

"Let's hurry. It's hard telling what they'll do to Julie."

"Think you can make it all right? You've got a pretty bad wound on the back of your head."

"Yah, I've got to be all right."

"Here, let me wrap something around your head to help stop the bleeding." Tom tore his shirt sleeve off, and secured it around Paul's head.

They arrived back at the ranch as fast as the horses could carry them. Paul felt dizzy and sick to his stomach, but he had to make it. He kept thinking of Julie out there some place, being carried off by some savage Redskins. He knew most of the Indians in the Northwest were pretty docile. Yet, sometimes liquor could generate them to play havoc on the white man. Some proved more of a nuisance than to be feared, desiring only to steal the white man's possessions.

Unfortunately, some renegades hated the white man with a passion. Many Indians were friendly, and tried to accept the fact that they should live on reservations, which the govern-

39

ment had "given them." But to some, being pushed off the only land they ever knew by pale-faced, overbearing people could not be received with approval. White men not only captured their land, but also killed their source of meat, and took over the lakes and rivers they had fished for centuries. The only retaliation they knew was to fight or they, their women and children would soon die off and disappear.

Tom related Paul and Julie's tragic experience to his father and youngest brother, while Mark dressed Paul's head wound, assuring them he would be all right, if he took it easy for a few days. Paul insisted that he go along, since he felt responsible for Julie. Tom saddled fresh horses and packed what food and supplies he felt they might need. In a rather brief amount of time they were back at the run-down cabin to trace the trail of the Indians and their captive.

Visible traces of several horses and footprints were discovered around the old deserted shack not really revealing how many Indians to deal with. As the four men followed the tracks on farther, they determined a small party had kidnapped Julie.

The McCalisters relied on their experience at tracking. Ranchers with cattle sometimes spend hours searching for strays, or wildcats, wolves or bear that oftentimes caused the death of both man and animal. These men had also gained skill at hunting for food, and deer, and elk, which were plentiful. They had enjoyed many a delicious meal of venison in the comfort of their home.

But, this search was different. They couldn't afford to waste any time. Darkness would settle in a couple of hours. With spring in the Northwest comes extended daylight hours, this being in their favor. Still, the density of the woods would cause darkness to engulf them more rapidly. As long as the Indians kept moving, they felt Julie would be safe. So they wanted to cover as much territory as possible before nightfall set in. The renegades would more than likely make camp then, too. Thick underbrush slowed them down considerably; several times they were led astray.

The Indians are an intelligent people. They knew this country well. Aware they would probably be trailed, the McCalisters found they had split up in different directions for a ways. Not knowing which trail to follow, of course, made tracking more difficult for the men. Farther on they would locate more tracks, as the Indians returned to the same party.

The sun slowly began its descent, disappearing behind towering, snow-tipped mountains. Twinkling stars filled the firmament. If only this would have been a full moonlit night, the men could have traveled further. But it wasn't. A full moon belonged to lovers, not tragedy. Finally, the men felt forced to make the decision to give up their search until sunrise.

Camp was set up alongside a narrow, gushing stream. Only a few words were spoken. Their faces appeared grim, tired and concerned. Joel made a pot of coffee on the open campfire and offered the steaming brew to his sons. "Here, take this. Maybe it will relieve some of the tension. Paul, how's your head feel?"

"I'll be all right, Pa. You always told me I had a hard head." His humor was obviously still intact.

Joel tried to smile.

"Wait! Listen! Do you hear anything?" Tom interrupted.

They all turned in the direction of Tom's voice, trying to listen with intense ears. "What do you hear, son?"

"I'm almost sure I can make out the sound of voices," he quietly answered, as he placed his ear to the ground; an old trick he had learned from an Indian friend. "I think I'll go scout around a while."

"All right. Don't take any unnecessary chances." His father now spoke in a whisper.

Tom's towering, iron physique disappeared into the

blackness of the night. Although a large, trim man, Tom learned from his previous hunting experiences to be light on his feet. While moving swiftly and quietly through the brush, he climbed to the crest of a hill to get a better view. The voices became more audible. After reaching the top he could peer down unseen. There below he spied a small party of Redskins grouped around a fire. Tom counted eight, possibly discussing what to do with their captive. Quite obviously they had been consuming the white man's liquor.

The Coast Indians were short, stocky people with slightly slanted eyes. Their legs became bowed from sitting in canoes and in squatting positions. Their skin was lighter than those of the south, and even from east of the Cascades. The Coast Indians had an unusual custom of flattening the head by fastening a heavy piece of leather or board to a baby's forehead. The head would then grow into a peaked shape, which explained the nickname, Flatheads, the white men had chosen to give them. In the summer months the Indian braves wore little or no clothing, although most wore a breechcloth. The women usually wore a short skirt of twisted bark or grass, extending to their knees, and caught at the waist by a cord. In the winter they wore robes of skins or blankets made from dog hair, and broad-brimmed hats woven from roots or bark. Some of the Indians rubbed on fish oil to help keep out the cold, which didn't leave behind a very pleasing aroma. Many of the Indians went barefoot the year round.

Tom's keen eyes searched around the campfire until he located the diminutive figure of a girl. She sat tied to a tree with her head hanging downward. He recognized her immediately. But . . . was she dead? What had they done? Had they already killed her? Oh, God! No! They can't be too late. Please, God, let her be alive!" Tom said in silent prayer.

He quietly made his way back down the hillside, and quickly ran back to the sight where his father and brothers waited eagerly for his return. Tom related what he had observed, and they set out to execute a plan, realizing they were outnumbered two to one. No doubt the Indians would wait until dawn to do anything, if they hadn't already. But they couldn't take that chance. They needed to work swiftly with a surprise attack. Possibly in the dark they could make the Indians believe there were more of them. At least the four decided it was worth a try, feeling the necessity to at least make the endeavor.

The men followed closely behind Tom as he led them to where he had located the Indian encampment, then split up, surrounding their enemies. They had been instructed to listen for Joel to make the first move.

"Eeee-yaaa-hoooo!" came out a terrifying cry. Then the explosive uprising commenced.

Four anxious men proceeded to dash back and forth in the black night, shouting their ear-piercing rifles into the air, while whooping and hollering. They hoped it would portray the sound of a whole Calvary present. In their drunken stupor the Indians must have rationalized that their gods must be punishing them. So frightened were they, not knowing which way to charge, and with the lessening of their reasoning from the liquor, the Indians kept running back and forth into each other. After a few wild moments the ordeal terminated. The Indians had escaped into the darkness, leaving their captive behind. The men didn't really want to kill them; an Indian uprising was the last episode they wished to encounter later on.

Finally, the rescuers ran to the center of where the action took place. Tom rushed to the bent over figure of the girl, while the others checked to make sure her abductors had fled out of sight.

"Is she alive?" Paul anxiously asked Tom.

"She's alive, thank God, but she's burning up with fever, and is still unconscious. Her clothes are damp."

43

"We'd better get her back to our camp, and wrap her in blankets until we can get her home. I'm afraid she may catch pneumonia," Mark stated.

Only a few hours later dawn's light broke through the thickness of the trees, and the exhausted party of five was directing their mounts toward the ranch. Julie was held in Joel's lap, while Paul pulled her horse by the reins alongside his mount. Mark rode on ahead to town for the doctor. Never before did home appear so inviting.

Julie had been unconscious through the whole ordeal, and didn't learn about the exciting rescue until the following afternoon. Not only did her four favorite men reclaim her from what possibly could have been a dreadful death, but she escaped the ravages of pneumonia as well. She was still acutely ill, but in a few days the doctor reported, "She should be up and about, taking care of her men again."

Paul, too, needed some extra care.

Numerous wild berries of the Washington Territory serve as a delight to its people. Strawberries set out to ripen into luscious red fruit around the middle of June, raspberries, blueberries, blackberries, and other varieties ripen somewhat later. Julie decided the enticing red strawberries would be a treat for her adopted family. After being confined to bed and not allowed to leave the house for days, one warm June day, with the morning duties completed, she felt determined to pick some of the wild berries for jam and shortcake.

Julie saddled up the sorrel mare, Scarlet, her loyal companion now, and rode some distance before spying the tiny plants sporting bright red berries intermingled with white dainty blossoms. Leaving the horse to graze nearby, she set out at filling her bucket. After a time of searching, and the bucket nearly half full, a strange feeling came over her being, as if someone was watching. Raising her head slowly, her body flinched upon discovering two pair of dark eyes peering into hers.

The piercing eyes belonged to those of two Indians. Julie recalled them being two of the Indians who had captured her a couple weeks earlier. Overwhelmed with fear, her hands grew clammy. Her heart felt as if it had jumped into her throat and began beating so rapidly, she knew they must hear the thumping sound. The frightened girl attempted a scream, but no sound would come from her mouth. With her stomach churning and knees weakening, she felt afraid of fainting.

She then realized the Indians appeared frightened, too. Yet they kept standing there motionless, just staring mystified, as if she was some product of their imagination. One of them extended an arm to touch her hair, then quickly retrieved it. Gradually the fear began to subside from Julie, causing her to become almost amused at these extraordinary people. Managing a smile, she then reached out the pail to offer them some of the freshly picked berries. Startled, they jumped backward, then ran off as if they had seen a spirit. Julie shook her head and just stood there, still alarmed, but thankful the trying experience appeared to be over. After regaining her composure, she mounted her horse, and rode back to the welcome sight of the ranch . . . grasping tightly to the prized bucket of berries.

That evening, rather reluctantly, Julie divulged the incident to the McCalisters. They reprimanded her in a protective, yet sympathetic manner for leaving the ranch. Feeling there should be no need for alarm, Joel went on to describe what he had learned about the people.

"The Indians are a superstitious culture. They believe everything in nature has a spirit, such as an animal, the sky, moon, stars, trees and so on. Most of the Indians of the Coast bury their dead above ground, usually in a canoe or box, which is put high up in a tree, or on a scaffold. Some leave them on the ground. Ornaments, usually broken first, and other property are buried with their dead. Sometimes even a horse or a slave is buried with them. Of course they believe these things can be used again in their spirit world. A dead slave or an unimportant person usually isn't buried. Instead their bodies are thrown into the woods or even into the ocean. It's possible, Julie," Joel went on to say, "that the Indians appeared awestruck by your hair. They probably had never seen a person with red hair before, and maybe thought you to be some unknown god. Especially since you survived the night of your capture. Above all, if you should happen to become aware of them again, hide your fear. The Indians admire a brave person."

Just the same, Julie had a restless sleep that night. Several days went by, and no more sightings of the Indians were seen. The incident soon became a part of the past.

In the meantime Julie had made some new friends. She enjoyed a delightful afternoon visiting the Judsons, on the day following the berry-picking incident. It didn't take long for her to become attached to Sarah's two younger sisters, Susie who just turned five, and Kaye the four-year-old. Sarah and Julie enjoyed taking the little girls to a nearby lake wading. Julie often read them stories with each visit. When time for her to leave, they gave her a big kiss on the cheek, and begged her to stay . . . just a little longer. Much of her spare moments were spent at the Judson ranch from then on.

One afternoon Emma Judson met Julie at the door, "I'm sorry, I'd better not let you in. Two of the children came down sick last night. We sent for Doc Rider early this morning. They have scarlet fever." Mrs. Judson looked pale and worn out from staying up several nights caring for her family.

"Are you sure I can't be of some help, Mrs. Judson? I'd be more than glad to do anything I can."

"I know you would dear, but Sarah and the older children

46

are helping to take care of whatever needs to be done. We don't want you to come down with it, too, but we do appreciate your offer." She smiled and slowly closed the door.

Several days later Doc Rider happened by the McCalister ranch with the sad news. Emma Judson had come down with the fever. The doctor did everything he could for her, but her body had become feeble, frail and run-down. By the end of the week, the smiling eyes slipped into a deep sleep, never to smile again in this world, as we know it. Everyone who had known the kind lady felt confident that she was in the divine care of her Maker. Emma Judson had succumbed to the fever.

Clouds of sorrow came upon the entire community. Emma was deeply loved by many. Her name would not be entered in history books as a great lady, but in the minds of those privileged to have known her, she would long be remembered. Emma had never been too busy to watch over the sick, extend her services as a midwife, even taking in children from time to time and embrace them with her love. Some of their parents had been found dead after an Indian raid, leaving the young ones as orphans, Susie and Kaye being two of them. When families found themselves unable to care for their own, Luke and Emma Judson always offered a helping hand.

The Judsons had settled on their land about the same time as the McCalisters, and several other families. They were pioneers in the true sense of the word—a courageous, unselfish breed of people with inner strengths and endearing hearts, always unashamed to lend their moral and physical support and unshaken faith. They contributed in preparing the west so others could follow; so others could live in a tamed land without fear and with a bright horizon.

After Emma's death, Sarah, being the oldest of the children, inherited the responsibilities and momentous task of household duties, as well as looking after her younger brothers and sisters. Luke Judson grieved his wife's death, and couldn't seem to accept the fact that his beloved wife was gone. Julie felt this an opportunity to repay Sarah and the Judsons for the wealth of human kindness they had shown to her.

Milking a cow often became a woman's job, so Julie decided she would help out by taking over the early morning chore, in this way she would still have plenty of time for her own household schedule. Today would be her first day.

"Good morning, Mr. Judson. I hope I'm not late," she spoke cheerfully.

"Right on time, young lady. Here are a couple of pails. Let's start our first lesson." Luke forced a smile. Julie noticed his thin face was drawn, his eyes sunken with dark circles under them.

They set their course in the direction of the barn, carrying several pails. Julie learned to her surprise the Judsons had ten milk cows. A large part of the milk, cream and butter the family used; some would be sold to the hotel in town for the diner; much of it was given to those less fortunate.

The short trip to the building housing the livestock created quite a scene, if one would arise early enough to observe it. At the head of the parade led Luke, carrying two arms full of stacked buckets. Julie followed close behind with her two buckets. Trailing her came two large dogs, three puppies, five cats, and at least a dozen furry kittens all accompanying their chosen leader in single file.

Mr. Judson dumped some oats in the trough at the first animal's head, pulled up a stool, sat down and placed one of the pails under the cow's bag. He began to hum a funny familiar tune, and proceeded with the first lesson. Julie looked on engrossed.

When the pail showed about half full, Luke looked up to his pupil and said, "How about you trying now, Julie?"

She sat down eagerly with her own empty bucket, *This looks easy,* she thought, grabbing a hold of the udders and squeezing. Nothing came out. She squeezed again, harder.

"Maaaooo . . ."

"Hey, you're not supposed to pull it off!" Luke almost grinned. "Here, you'd better let me show you again. See, you squeeze and pull down in a rhythmic motion. Now try again. Hum a tune. They like music, and it'll help you get in rhythm."

"Ah, ha, there . . . I knew I could do it," when the squirt of milk plunked to the bottom of the pail, gradually increasing to a stream. Mr. Judson left her to her milking and started on one of the other cows, while she kept up her humming and squeezing.

"Ohhh!" A tail swished in her face.

Now and then Julie would look up from her pail and observe Mr. Judson squirting some milk in the mouth of one of the eager onlookers. First one cat then another sat enjoying their treat, till all the small animals felt full and leaned back to wash their faces with their paws, pleasingly contented. By the time Luke milked the other nine cows, Julie had her bucket maybe three quarters full.

"I . . . a . . . guess I didn't do so good." She sat up straight, rubbing her tired hands.

"You'll do all right once you get the hang of it. Just like anything else, it takes practice. Here, let me finish up. No use overworking yourself the first day," he chuckled.

As Julie started to get up from the stool, the animal moved to one side. Sure enough it had to be Julie's side. She lost her balance, tripped over the stool, which in turn tripped over the pail of milk on top of the startled girl. Now Mr. Judson was usually a very quiet reserved person. Julie had never heard him talk very much, and never could she recall him laughing, but he was now. He tried at first to restrain himself; only he couldn't hold it in any longer. He laughed so hard that the tears started to roll down his cheeks.

At first Julie felt miserably disgusted with herself. With the exception of seeing this man finding some merriment in the situation, it became almost worth such a regrettable scene she had enacted.

Sarah and several of the younger children heard the commotion coming from the barn by this time, and ran from the house to investigate. There they found Julie sprawled out on the floor, milk soaked, with the overturned bucket and stool lying nearby. Both she and their father sat doubled over in stitches, transforming grief-laden eyes into tears of laughter.

Finally, they all went into the house. Julie changed into one of Sarah's dresses, making herself presentable once again and said her good-byes. She would be back in the morning, if they were still willing to put up with her. Actually, she left with a feeling of satisfaction; she had helped bring back an unexpected little joy into her dear friends' lives.

As she started to set the breakfast table for the morning meal of her family, a little later than usual, Joel asked how her first day went on the new job opportunity.

"Okay, Papa Mack (the name she had given him sometime ago). They want me back," Julie managed to say, concealing a smile. "Although I may just feed the chickens next time."

Four

It was the year 1876, the Centennial year for the United States of America. A year to celebrate one hundred memorable years of independence from our mother country of England. With the Fourth of July drawing near, and even though the Territory of Washington had not as yet been accepted as one of the United States, the dream still filled the minds of its inhabitants. A day of festivities was being planned in the growing settlement of Seattle. Many of the sojourners from the eastern states occupied the uncivilized western territory, some not sure if they wanted to be a permanent resident; nevertheless, they had a desire to take part in their country's celebration.

A parade, rodeo, and a street dance, concluding with fireworks over the Puget Sound waters of scenic Elliot Bay, were the festivities being proposed for the momentous day. Everyone in the surrounding area able to attend ardently awaited the excitement of this inspiring event in the well-known township given the nickname, the new New York.

Among those who envisioned the nearly thirty-mile trek to the location of the grand affair were the McCalisters. They arranged to take several days out of their busy schedule to join fellow citizens, leaving a faithful few ranch hands in charge of the homestead.

Joel conducted the long drive in the old buckboard, which had been converted into a covered wagon. Julie sat beside him, overflowing in exuberance. The brothers rode alongside the wagon on horseback over the well-worn trail.

An early morning sun helped invigorate the refreshing scent of evergreens. To the east the snow-covered Cascade mountains and grandeur of proud Mt. Rainier captured the view now and again. A powerful team of horses pulled the wagon over hills, alongside rocky ridges and winding rivers, through a clearing sprinkled with a profusion of wild flowers tinted in vivid shades of reds, blues, purples and yellows. To the west one could view snow-clad Mt. Olympus, standing out somewhat taller than the rest of the peaks in the towering Coast Mountain range.

Ever so often Joel pointed out rectangular lodges built by Indians, who used them as winter dwellings. Some were from forty to a hundred feet in length, and from fifteen to twice that in breadth; each, he had learned, housed several families. The Indians, he explained to Julie, used cedar logs for construction, because the red cedar proved easier to split into planks with their crude instruments. Down the center of a lodge would run a shallow trough in which fires could be made; smoke would escape through openings in the roof. Platforms or bunks were formed for sleeping along the walls for family members. Often sacred totem poles stood guard near the village to chase off evil spirits. In the summer months portable lodges of mats or skins, the teepees, could be seen for use in hunting or berry picking expeditions.

The tired travelers finally reached the outskirts of their destination. Seattle was a bustling town with only a small overcrowded hotel. The McCalisters came prepared for camping out. They discovered one lonely tree growing not far off the trail on an unsettled plot of land clothed in deep rich, green grass to house their wagon and tired animals for a few days at the edge of the settlement. After setting up camp for the night, following supper and visiting around the campfire for a while, the men fixed their sleeping gear out under the glistening stars. Julie found comfort inside the wagon on a soft feather mattress they had prepared for her. Although noise from the saloons grew more and more boisterous, she soon drifted off to sleep, glad that "her" men didn't join the hubbub in the taverns.

With the sun's warm rays announcing another new day, Julie lazily arose from her comfortable quarters, poured some cool water from a pail into the oval basin she had brought along, and sponged her body. Outside the wagon unfamiliar voices were heard. When she peered out the front opening, to her amazement, she found several more families in wagons had joined them during the night. Safety in numbers is always a good policy, and she was pleased to have another opportunity to meet some new acquaintances.

Following breakfast, the men strolled into town to find what contests they could enter for the rodeo later on in the day, while the women cleaned up the campsites and donned their latest fashions. Anticipating the event, Julie had spent many hours sewing a long full skirt of red and white gingham. She wore a blouse of white with full three-quarter-length sleeves, over it a royal blue vest. Her shiny red hair was tied at the neck by a large red ribbon.

While meandering into town, Julie found many displays of beautiful handmade quilts, all sorts of intricate samplers, knitted garments, crocheted doilies and items of tatting on sale. A number of fruit stands, scrumptious pastries, and home canned goods filled tables lined along the earthen walkways. Busy admiring all the impressive merchandise, she didn't notice a handsome young man walking toward her.

"Good morning, ma'am. I'm Bob Randal. Are you looking for anything or anyone in particular?" He greeted with a southern drawl and friendly smile. "May I be of help?"

She politely returned the smile. "Yes, I am looking for my family, the McCalisters. Do you know them?"

"No, sorry, ma'am. Can't say that I do. But it's hard to

imagine anyone keeping a lovely lady like you waiting." His green eyes twinkled.

Julie walked over to the nearest vacant bench and seated herself, prepared to wait. The young man followed. About the moment he sat down, Julie noticed one of the McCalisters strolling down the well-occupied street. Slightly relieved, she excused herself and went over to greet Tom, sticking her arm in his possessively.

"Good morning. Have you been in town long?" he asked, somewhat surprised by her actions.

"No, just a few minutes. I've been enjoying all the exhibits. It's a lovely morning. Already warm, isn't it?" She smiled up at him, turning her head barely enough to catch a glimpse of the stranger out of the corner of her eye.

"The parade is about to begin. Let's find a good spot to watch it." Tom appeared nervous.

Julie glanced over and smiled sweetly at her new acquaintance, still sitting on the bench. Tom strengthened his hold on her arm, as they weaved in and around the expectant crowd.

At the head of the parade a man in a dark blue uniform marched, clutching a pole holding the celebrated flag of stars and stripes. A civilian followed, carrying the territorial flag. Next, a small provincial band played a variety of favorite tunes, such as "Yankee Doodle," "Dixie," and more. A huge statue of the legendary Paul Bunyan and his renowned ox, Babe, were tied onto carts pulled by jovial clowns, delighting young and old alike with their silly antics and painted faces. Descendants of the prestigious and loved Indian, Chief Seattle, and several members of his tribe proceeded in their colorful regalia, some on foot and others mounted on brightly decorated horses. A small Calvary of horsemen in navy blue uniforms concluded the parade. The long awaited day of jubilee and celebration had begun.

An animated crowd moved its way to the outskirts of

town, where the rodeo was the next event on the agenda. Wooden stands quickly filled to capacity, leaving many standing. Joel had joined Julie, and to their delight, were able to locate seats on the top row of the platform. Tom had joined his two brothers. They had signed up to be contenders in different entries of the gala affair. Soon an announcer entered the center of the arena, surrounded by corrals on three sides; the stand on the remaining. He welcomed the audience to the flourishing town of Seattle and to the special significance of such a jubilant occasion being honored today.

From the middle of the arena the announcer shot a blast from his pistol initiating the action of the wild, dangerous, yet thrilling rodeo, as he hurried out of the way. The calf roping contest provided the beginning of the exciting sport, when out from one shoot vaulted a horse and rider. A calf darted out from another. After several participants ventured their turn, the winner's name was announced, Robert Randal. Next the bull-dogging contest took place, then wild bronco riding. Time slipped away so swiftly, as one shaken contestant after another shook the dust off his clothes, while leaving the focal point of the arena. A few had to be carried off, and unfortunate but expected part of the daring exhibition of skill and chance.

Each time a winner was revealed, Robert Randal's name ranked at the head of the list, much to the astonishment of a certain female spectator. However, Paul McCalister had been recorded claiming second place in the bull riding contest. Joel and Julie enjoyed watching the hilarious wild-cow milking competition. It brought back amusing memories to Julie, even though a much calmer animal accompanied her milking day.

Now, the time for the five-mile race scheduled the thrilling close to the rodeo portion of the day with a stake being one thousand dollars. Twenty anxious horsemen on their swiftest breeds filled the line up . . . blacks, sorrels, bays and paints, to name a few. The most excellent horses in the territory, groomed to perfection, manifested their desire to reveal their talents. The rugged course crossed rocky streams and ravines, led up steep hills and down into rich, green meadows, making its way back through town, and on to the rodeo grounds.

A loud explosive noise from a gun filled the air once again. Immediately the race electrified the audience. Cheers rang out from the well-wishers, each one rooting for their favorite contestant. Necks strained while they watched one horse and rider then another disappear down a hill and back into view. Julie jumped up and down, yelling her excitement, as Joel watched equally amused at her and always eager to observe superb horsemanship displayed. Not to mention the fact that his three sons had taken part in the race. Soon the riders were completely out of sight, hidden by the ancient forest.

"There they are!" someone yelled, when several riders could be seen emerging in the distance once again racing toward the finish line. It was difficult to distinguish which horse held the lead. A golden palomino followed the two blacks closely. As they drew closer, Joel recognized Tom on one of the black horses. The other was the young man who had captured the talk of the crowd, Robert Randal. Both were encouraging their mounts on for the win of this most prestigious event of the rodeo. High overhead the bright sun released its brilliant warm rays to those below. Sweat poured from the animals' bodies as well as their riders. The two black horses stretched neck and neck, each straining for the lead. Wild cheers thundered from the overzealous crowd, as horse and rider plunged toward the finish line.

The winner proved to be the magnificent black with a white star on its forehead, and four white stocking hooves. Swarms of excited admirers scurried over to capture a glimpse of the exhausted horse and its proud rider, and share their congratulations. Yes, Tom's face shone with pride, as he stroked his splendid stallion, then managed to slide down from his saddle to greet many well-wishers and close challenger.

"Well, I reckon that is probably the closest race I have ever been a part of. That's a mighty fine horse you have there," drawled the light-haired Bob Randal. "I don't suppose you'd sell him?" He knew what the answer would be, as he grinned.

"Thanks, but no thanks. It's the first big race I've entered him in. He really amazed me, too. I knew he could outrun any horse on our ranch, but I wasn't sure how he'd do in a genuine race," Tom replied.

About that time Joel and Julie managed their way through the crowd to congratulate their winner.

"Why, hello there, ma'am. I was wondering when I'd run into the most exquisite lady of this here territory again," said the outspoken Mr. Randal, exposing his teeth in a smile.

Julie's face began to turn an attractive crimson tint, while releasing a timid hello.

"Do you know Julie?" Tom asked.

"Sort of. I introduced myself to this lovely lady earlier this morning. You say your name is Julie? That's a mighty purdy name, ma'am."

Julie just smiled shyly. *He obviously enjoyed embarrassing her,* Julie thought.

Joel sensed Julie's embarrassment. "I'm Joel McCalister." He reached forth his hand to shake the other man's. "Why don't we all head over to the picnic grounds and get in on some of that excellent food I've been hearing about? Won't you join us, Mr. Randal?"

"I'd be mighty pleased. Thank you kindly, sir."

The four of them sauntered on toward the picnic area. Julie stayed close to the two McCalister men, a little disconcerted that Papa Mack would invite this forward stranger, who made her feel so uneasy; although, he was rather pleasing to the eye with his curly blond hair and exciting green eyes. His tall slender frame stood perhaps even a little taller than Tom, and his broad, very masculine shoulders . . . but . . . still . . . he was very forward. *Too forward,* thought Julie, while she pretended not to notice him.

"Looks like the line starts down there."

"Hmm. Oh, yes." Julie followed along behind Tom and the other men. Everyone had brought food and had added their contribution to the dozens of tables already covered with an abundance of hams, wild turkey, venison, roasts, casseroles, salads, and appetizing dishes of all kinds. Soon, Julie had filled her plate to the brim, since she couldn't resist trying one delicious dish after another. The victuals appeared too succulent to worry about the figure today. *Eating someone else's cooking always seems to be better than your own,* Julie thought, even though she was becoming a much better cook by now.

The small party of four found shade under a clump of trees overlooking the bay, the sun glimmering across the blue, green water. In the distance the snow-capped Olympics and forests of tall, green firs and cedars contrasted with the deep, blue sky and puffy, white clouds, while they drifted ever so slowly by in the realm above. A slight breeze off the Sound felt good. This had been a wonder filled day with still more attractions to come.

"What dreams are you gathering in that sweet head?" Paul broke into her wonderland, as he and Mark joined the group.

"Oh, hi, Paul . . . Mark. I'm just enjoying the beautiful scenery, while sitting here stuffing my face. What an exciting day this has been!" Julie motioned for Paul to sit down beside her, while making room for him in between Bob Randal and herself.

"Do you know Mr. Randal?"

"I reckon everyone knows Mr. Randal after the rodeo today," smiled Paul. "How do you do there?" His strong arm grasped that of the other man's outstretched hand.

"My pleasure, Paul. You didn't do so bad out there yourself."

"How do you like our part of the world?"

"Ya'll have some magnificent country here. Course it can't compare with Texas, but then, I reckon Texas can't compare with the Washington Territory either."

They all chuckled.

"Do you plan on staying up here in these parts?" Joel McCalister joined in the conversation.

"Yes, sir." After a pause, "I'm the new sheriff of a small town just east of here."

An amazed expression came over Julie's face. "A sheriff?"

"Yes, ma'am. I suppose you've heard of the town of Cascadia?"

"Oh, yeh. I heard we were getting us a sheriff . . . like the big cities," smiled Tom.

"So you're from Cascadia," he turned to Julie's direction, displaying those perfect white teeth. "I needed some money to tide me over while I find a place to live. That's why I entered the rodeo contests," commented Randal.

The sun began its descent hiding behind the mountains, releasing vivid coral and golden tones while fading into a lavender summer sky. Soon the colors grew fainter and vanished into the darkness. A full moon began to emerge, illuminating a pathway for the multitudes of people gathering along the shore, while locating places to sit in anticipation for the fireworks being prepared. Eventually, a blast was heard, and an explosion of sparkling colors began to fill the waiting sky, challenging the multitude of stars in their brilliance. The effervescent splendor reflected in the water, as one radiant color after another sprinkled to the earth below. The ooo's and aahh's, especially from the children, could be heard all around.

As the last of the fireworks faded, soft music began to infiltrate the air, reminding those who cared of the street dance soon to begin. Tired youngsters were tucked in their knapsacks, appeased by the excitement of the day. The McCalister clan joined the joyful crowd, chattering and laughing as they proceeded toward the direction of the music. Indeed, the celebration was not yet over, while couples began to swing to the rhythm of the instruments.

Julie had been extremely quiet this evening. "Are you having a good time?" Joel asked somewhat concerned.

"Oh, yes, Papa Mack."

"It appears something is bothering you?" Joel wasn't quite convinced. He had noticed her eyeing the crowd and peering over her shoulder several times.

"I've had a wonderful day, really I have," Julie said.

Paul then asked her to dance, and they soon disappeared in the midst of the throng of people.

It seemed only minutes had drifted by when the notes of "The Star Spangled Banner" began to fill the air. Gradually, the people started to join in singing the words, as they gathered around the flag of stars and stripes. A tear fell down the cheek of one individual and then another. A star spangled banner, not merely just a cloth hanging from a pole to be caught up into the wind, but a symbol of hearts that have given and will give their lives for a country they claim as their own. A symbol representing people who strive for freedom and justice, love, and above all . . . peace. A peace that includes all men and women no matter what their background, or race, and peace with God Almighty.

The Centennial Celebration had come to a conclusion . . . one hundred years of independence that had not come without cost. An exciting commemoration was over, but lives of the people who took part were not. A lifetime remained with victories to be won. Washington was still merely a territory, and not yet one of the United States. But after tonight a living dream of visions were being planted, which one day they felt confident would become a reality.

The days away from the ranch seemed like weeks. So much had happened to fill hearts with enjoyment. The thirty-mile trek to Cascadia and the McCalister ranch ended much too soon; tomorrow the everyday chores would be there. Still, it's satisfying to be home in your own comfortable bed with familiar surroundings. But then, as Julie thought, *Where really is my home?* Somewhere out there in the darkness Julie had a home. Where?

She twisted the golden band she still wore on her left hand. Is there someone wondering where she was? Did she leave "him," or was it "them"? Could there possibly be a child?

"Dear God, help me remember," Julie prayed for the first time since she had come to live with the McCalisters over two months ago. "I've got to know," Julie said to herself, as she tightened her eyes, finally drifting into an exhausted sleep.

Something had happened to her during the eventful journey. Something that aroused the young woman's feelings, disturbing her with an uneasiness that filled her with a desire to become aware of just who she was, and what kind of life she had left behind.

Five

A change had come over Julie. Joel McCalister sensed that something appeared to be bothering her ever since the celebration a couple weeks ago. She seemed different in some way, not quite as vivacious as usual, more withdrawn, and often kept more to herself. He wanted to talk with her; still, he was determined not to intrude in the young woman's privacy, so he decided to wait for her to come to him.

Mark made a decision to transfer from Whitman College in eastern Washington to the Territorial University in Seattle. This would enable him to be closer to his family and loved ones, if needed, and be able to come home for holidays. During the summer Mark and Sarah realized their love for each other, but decided to wait until he finished his two more years of schooling before making any wedding plans. Sarah accepted the need for her presence at home until her younger brothers and sisters could assume more responsibilities on the farm. Her father depended so much on her; gradually, he was coming out of the shell he had crawled into when Emma died.

Excitement mixed with tenderness filled the atmosphere the day Mark left for school. Sarah planned a farewell party for him the night before. When the time arrived to say good-bye, the words started to swell up in Joel's throat. Feeling proud of his youngest son, he knew that one day Mark would make a fine doctor. But good-byes tempt feelings of loneliness for those left behind, and his son would be deeply missed.

The following evening after the family had retired for bed and the fire slowly turned into hot coals, Joel stayed behind, sitting in his large overstuffed chair pondering the thoughts of the day, when he heard the door to Julie's room open.

"Is that you, Papa Mack?"

"Yes, dear, can't you sleep?"

"No, sir." After a time of hesitation, "There's something I've been meaning to talk to you about for a while."

"Come, sit down here, child," replied the older man, while he pulled up a chair by the fire and added a log to the dwindling embers. Soon it began to crackle again, as he poked at the red coals. It really wasn't a cold evening. But, winter or summer, Joel's favorite time to relax and think through the day's happenings was sitting by a slow, burning fire after his family had retreated to their own rooms.

He didn't try to pressure Julie into talking, although he was anxious for what he might find pressing on her heart. Patience portrayed a virtue he learned from his lovely Mattie many years ago. He discovered if he waited long enough, people usually have a need for pouring out the concerns of the mind. He also found some individuals felt a need to talk with Joel McCalister when troubled. They knew he would devote to them his listening ear and perhaps even share some profound wisdom.

Julie gazed into the glowing fire. After a few minutes she looked up into the face of this dear friend she had grown to rely on like a father. "I earnestly want you to know how grateful I am for the kindness you and your sons have shown me, Papa Mack. And I long for you to understand what I am about to say. I have been giving this a great deal of thought, and I've finally reached a decision." She paused a few seconds, peering into the blaze with the light reflecting in her hair. The room

63

permeated the silence except for the snapping of the burning logs now and then.

Not raising her head, Julie spoke again, "I feel I must go away for a while." The words came hard for her, while trying to hide her emotions. But the tears, though hidden, were there within reach. "My feelings for each of you have been so filled with an immense love, and I've felt so much a part of this home you have shared with me . . . that I feel I must leave," Julie finally said.

"At the Fourth of July Celebration I came to realize how essential it is to know just who I am. I could stay here and be forever happy, except for this wedding band I have on my finger. I feel it necessary to know who was a part of my past, and who my family really is. Do you understand, Papa Mack?"

"I believe I do, Julie. And under the same circumstances, I'm sure I would have the same feelings, a desire to know my past. Let's not get too hasty though. Where would you go? There's no reason you should have to leave this only home you know right now. Let's see if we can't work this matter out together." Joel's voice had a calming effect on his listener.

For the first time in days, Julie felt a release of anxiety replaced by an inner peace of assurance, taking possession of her soul. She really didn't want to leave the safety of this loving family; but she was becoming too attached, and that seemed to frighten her. If she could only remember her past, maybe things would materialize into a satisfactory solution.

"Thank you, Papa Mack. I just don't want to be a burden to you."

"Don't be concerned about that, my dear. If anything, you've been a help and a blessing at a time I needed you most. I'll start inquiring tomorrow. I know some people who might be of help. You go back to bed now and get some rest. Don't worry. We'll work things out together."

Julie enjoyed a restful sleep for the first time in a multitude of days.

Joel rode into town the following morning. He found the new sheriff's office completed, and upon entering the building, found Bob Randal sitting at a large desk going over some papers. After hearing Joel's footsteps at the door, he said, "Come in. May I be of service to you, Mr. McCalister, I believe? Here have a seat." He motioned to a wooden chair.

The older man accepted his offer, then related his reason for being there and the few details he knew about Julie. After an hour of conference, Joel left and went about his other business while in town.

A couple days passed before there was a knock on the front door at the ranch. "Good morning, Miss Julie. I'm Sheriff Randal. Do you remember me?" His smile was genuine, yet business-like.

"Why, yes, Mr. Randal. Please come in. Papa Mack told me he had spoken with you. Have you learned anything yet?"

"No, I'm sorry. This may take some time, but I wanted you and Mr. McCalister to know I've sent some telegrams around, and hope to receive some kind of response soon," he answered, as he sat down on a kitchen chair.

"Julie . . . uh, do you mind if I call you Julie?"

"No, of course not, Mr. . . . er Sheriff Randal. Not at all."

"Then please call me Bob. I'd like to be your friend. I want you to tell me everything you can about those three men you were running from. Try to picture them in your mind . . . anything that would help us."

"I, I've tried so hard to forget. But I'll make an attempt. One was heavyset with a bushy beard and long dark hair," she began. "Let's see, I believe he had a scar over one eyebrow. He's the one that did all the talking. He was very angry and loud and extremely rude. I felt frightened and kept wishing he would just quiet down and leave me alone. The others . . . I, I can't remember . . . they just seemed to do whatever that large, barbaric man told them. But they, too, were big and grimy. I can remember . . . the smell . . . oohh," Julie broke off sobbing.

About that time Tom entered the room. "What's going on here? Why's Julie crying?" he asked angrily.

"It's all right, Tom. He's just trying to help me remember," Julie managed to say through her tears.

"I'm sorry. I didn't intend to upset or cause her to cry. I think that's enough for today, Julie." The sheriff apologized, somewhat embarrassed.

Tom poured each one a cup of coffee and gave Julie a hug.

"We're going to get to the bottom of this, Julie. I promise." The sheriff gave her a reassuring smile.

Several days went by. Julie and Sarah made plans to take the small children on a picnic before the summer was completely spent. The warm August afternoon air felt refreshing after a week of hardy, but needed rain. Julie had been canning some plums and peaches from the small orchard on the ranch. The wild blackberries had started ripening and her desire had been to make some jams and jellies for the family. But instead, today was going to be a day of pleasure.

She had prepared sandwiches, fruit and goodies, and loaded them into the buckboard. As she started to get into the wagon, a strange feeling urged her to go back and get the rifle Paul had been teaching her how to shoot.

A short distance from the Judson ranch, she could hear the excited voices of Susie, Kaye and the eight-year-old twins, Danny and David, hollering for her to hurry up. They were ready for an outing. It took only a moment for Sarah to appear at the door, carrying her contribution to the picnic. She also looked forward to spending some time with her friend. After everything and everyone found a place in the wagon, off they started on their merry trek.

Warm rays from the sun felt good, as they rode along the well beaten trail toward Mineral Lake, a favorite location of the populace. They spied a huge shady tree and decided it to be a perfect spot for the children to play, while Julie and Sarah set out the lunch. They spread a well-worn blanket on the velvet, green grass overlooking the serene, blue lake. The boys already found rocks to throw over the water to see who could strike the tree stump jutting out of the lake, while the girls had fun trying to catch butterflies and ladybugs.

"Time to eat," Sarah called after a while. The children came running, exaggerating how hungry their stomachs felt. The chicken and egg salad sandwiches tasted delicious, along with potato salad, homemade pickles, apple juice and cupcakes.

"Is everyone full?" Julie asked the little brood. They all responded with a firm, "Yes."

"How about us going on a treasure hunt?" They all agreed enthusiastically.

"I've made up a list of things for each one to find," Julie handed Sarah an empty basket. "Sarah, why don't you take Susie and David, and I'll take Kaye and Danny? We'll all meet back at the buckboard in one half hour, okay?"

The items were all objects that would be easy for the youngsters to find. What a great time they had searching for pretty rocks, grasshoppers, wild flowers, blackberries and such. As Julie started to head her team back towards the buckboard where they had decided to meet, there was a frightening scream from the opposite direction. Startled, she automatically rushed to the wagon and grabbed the rifle that was hid under the seat.

Sarah ran towards her with an expression of panic on her face. The two little ones were being hurried close on either side of her. "What's wrong?" Julie yelled. Immediately the terror was seen without an explanation needed. A large, black, growling bear followed too close behind them. Julie shot the rifle in the air, still the enormous animal kept charging forward. She didn't want to kill it, but in desperation had no choice. Saying a quick prayer, she aimed the rifle and pulled the trigger. Amazingly the bear collapsed in its tracks. She pulled the trigger one more time to be sure her aim had hit its mark. Motioning the children to stay at a distance, both young women ran over to the animal to verify whether it truly lie dead. It was. With a sigh of relief, they decided now was a good time to end their treasure hunt.

Just then Susie began pointing and screaming, "There's another one."

The older girls quickly glanced in the little girl's direction and indeed saw not one, but two small cubs running their way. "Oh, no! I've killed their mother," Julie exclaimed. Tears began to flow down her cheeks.

"You had to. She thought us to be a threat to her babies. She would have killed us." Sarah tried to comfort and reassure her.

"I guess you're right. But we can't leave those little cubs here without their mother. They may die. Let's see if we can catch them and take them back home with us."

It wasn't an easy task. They did manage to capture the untamed animals with some rope found in the buckboard. After tying them behind the wagon, they set out for home a very slow pace. The children were enormously exuberant over the eventful day, proclaiming the playful bears as the best part of their treasure hunt.

When back at the Judson ranch, Mr. Judson felt it was not the best idea to raise two little bear cubs with all the work he had to do in raising ten children and all. So, Julie offered to take the animals home with her. She wasn't sure they would get any better reception. Yet, she wanted to try. The children had lamented so over their sorrowful disappointment, when they couldn't keep them as their own pets.

As she approached the McCalister ranch, Paul and Tom waved, then yelled simultaneously, "What in the world do you have following behind?" Their faces shone full of bewilderment, like . . . what is she doing now?

"Well, you see, Sarah, the kids and I went on a picnic, and this big, black bear came charging at us, and I had to shoot it, and these little cubs soon came looking for their mother, and we just couldn't leave them there to starve or be killed by some other wild animal, and Mr. Judson said he didn't want them, and the children wanted them so much, so you see, I just had to bring them home, and . . . well . . . do you think Papa Mack will let me raise them? . . . Huh?"

"Whoa! You say you shot a bear?" exclaimed Paul. "I must have been a pretty good teacher."

Joel found refusing Julie anything very difficult. He had grown to love this young woman as his own flesh and blood. But, two bear cubs! Now there has to be a limit somewhere!

The little animals took to the fenced in pen Paul had made for them real well, at a distance from the other stock. They soon became pets to everyone, even for Joel. What a sight it was for him to watch the cubs, Julie, and the Judson children romping together. One day he even found Julie and the bears in the kitchen getting into the honey jar, wondering which ones were covered with more honey, Julie or the bears. She hadn't really intended for the cubs to come into the house, she tried to explain. But all of a sudden, there they were. She was trying to coax them outside by tempting them with the honey jar.

Julie and Sarah had become very close and enjoyed their friendship. The bear cubs were growing and getting harder to control and keep to their pen. The smaller Judson children came to play with them as often as they could, but the wild cubs played pretty rough at times, so the thrill of having a bear as their friend wasn't as exciting as in the beginning.

Joel knew as they grew bigger the bears would have to be set free sooner or later, he would tackle that problem when the time come, he decided. For now, why not enjoy the little gifts of laughter God gives you when they arise? What a change had come into his life since Mattie had died and this new person had captured his heart. He only wished Mattie could be here to share in such a joy.

His thoughts were interrupted by the shrill screams of, "Fire! Fire!" He looked up and saw flames coming from the barn with Julie in hysterics.

Although the fire was extinguished before much damage had been accomplished, Julie started crying, "I've gotta get her out! She's still in there! Help . . . oh . . . help!"

"It's all right, Julie. The fire's out. No one was hurt," Tom tried to console her.

"But she's in there. She's sick in bed. We've gotta get her out!" She kept pulling on his arm. Her huge dark eyes were glazed and overcome with fear.

"No one's in there. Everything's all right, Julie." Tom tried his best to assure the girl.

Then she collapsed into his arms. He carried her limp body into the house to her room and placed her gently on the bed.

Later that evening Julie wandered into the living room, where the three men were trying to relax and sort out the events that happened earlier. As she entered, the expression on her face was full of bewilderment. "Where . . . where am I? . . ." she stammered. "What happened?"

"There was a fire, but everything is okay. A kerosene lantern had been knocked over and caught some straw on fire in the barn. It was extinguished before causing any real damage. Don't you remember?" Joel patiently explained.

"It's like a nightmare. I remember a fire. I can't remember why, but I know someone is in the building."

"Who, Julie? Can you remember who?" one of the men urged her on.

"It's too frightening. I don't want to know!" She started to cry, overwhelmed with grief.

"Okay, honey. Calm down. We won't press you," Joel tried to calm her.

She wandered back to her room. The men were confused and wondered what they could do to help her.

"I need to go into town for some household supplies, Papa Mack," Julie mentioned at breakfast several days later.

"No problem. I'll hitch up the team to the buckboard," Tom offered. "It looks like it will be a nice day for you. I'd go along, but I need to check the fences today." Everyone was relieved that Julie was back to her normal self again.

"That's all right. Thanks for the offer. I'd like to leave as soon as I clean up the kitchen. Can I get anything for any of you? Also, I thought of buying some material for a new dress."

"Nothing for me, only the supplies you need today. Buy anything you want. You certainly have earned it with all the work you provide around here . . . keeping the house sparkling clean, washing our clothes and cooking. You've been a real blessing to us since Mattie died." Papa Mack's answer portrayed much sincerity.

"I love to do those things. Makes me feel wanted and needed, Papa Mack, and also a part of this wonderful family."

Soon Julie set out on the route to town. She found the trip enjoyable, giving her time to reflect on all God's goodness that he had shown to her in so many ways. It's not easy to start life over, when you lose your memory. Although, we find God works with us through the mysterious challenges, promising He will not give us more than we can bear. Sometimes during the struggle one wonders how life can ever go on without those we love. When we are open to Him, we find God does carry us along the highway of life, while paving the way, if we'll only learn to follow His signs of direction. In His strength a person can ford the roughest of rivers; and sometimes along the path He sends us caring angels in disguise, such as the McCalisters.

The earthen road into town winds through evergreen forests and luxurious meadows of green displaying a kaleidoscope of wild flowers. Up and over the hills the road climbs and crosses timber bridges that vibrate the clickety clacking sound of horses' hoofs, while mountain fresh streams sneak lazily under the wooden structures. Cotton, white clouds filled the bright blue sky overhead, as she strolled by on this pleasant day.

It's a good thing the horses know the way to town, when my mind wanders so. Julie had traveled many miles in thought.

Mrs. Jones had become a real friend to Julie when ordering supplies, since she had much more experience, and became the source the townsfolk put their trust in. She had become a widow several years back, and enjoyed her place of business that helped keep her mind occupied, often listening to her customers' problems. The general store, being the only one in the small town, exhibited an overabundance of goods to choose from. Her husband had left her well taken care of. Their four children had grown and moved away to nearby towns and occupations. While she endeavored to accumulate the items for her shopper, Julie mulled over the jewelry collection. Aw, something caught her eyes. An inspiring article she knew had to be fashioned just for her. Gently she picked it up and examined it closely . . . an emerald necklace similar to the one their mother had treasured and worn so often.

"It's perfect!" Julie excitedly showed Mrs. Jones, explaining how it reminded her of her mother's. "I've just got to buy it. I'll always cherish it."

Soon the wagon was loaded with the many purchases by the lady's assistant, Jake. Just as Julie started to climb onto the buckboard, she couldn't help but notice some men coming out of the saloon across the street. Three very boisterous men obviously had imbibed too much of the spiritous beverage, and were creating quite a noisy scene.

Instantaneously, she realized who they were, when the large hulky man turned in her direction. The scar over his eye and the unkempt bearded face was unmistakably the one who instigated the torching of her home and taking the lives of her parents. Her heart leaped into her throat causing it to constrict. Her hands became cold and clammy and began to tremble. Instinctively, she quickly turned away, trying to hide behind the wagon in hopes they wouldn't recognize her. Presently they mounted their horses, and to her relief, rode off in the opposite direction from which she would be heading.

Slowly she managed to make her way back inside the store. Mrs. Jones noticed the young woman and hurried towards her. "What in the world is the matter, my dear? Your face is colorless. Have you seen a ghost?"

"I, I'm sure I just saw the three men who killed my parents and burned our home."

"What? Come sit down." Mrs. Jones helped the trembling girl to a chair. "I'll get you a glass of water." Soon she was back. "Here, take this. Where did you see them? Are they still in town?" She nervously continued asking questions.

"They rode off west of town. Oh, I need to talk to the sheriff," the color in her face slowly returned, but her hands still remained shaky.

"I'm sorry. The sheriff has business out of town for a few days. I'll get Jake to ride his horse alongside your wagon till you get back home, unless you'd rather stay here for a while?"

"That won't be necessary. I'll be all right." Julie smiled, not wanting to cause her any more trouble.

The big man, Jake, insisted on escorting her until nearly reaching the ranch house, then felt it safe enough to leave her alone and head on back to town.

Julie told the men at suppertime what had happened. Tom was ready to take out after them, but Joel convinced him to wait until the sheriff returned and let him handle the situation. He made Julie promise to not leave the ranch, even to go to the Judsons for two or three days, so she would be under their shield of protection. Joel decided to get one of the ranch hands to ride over to the Judsons ranch and explain why she wouldn't be there for a few days to perform her regular chores in the mornings, so they wouldn't worry why she hadn't come.

Everything appeared to be going so well. Why did they have to show up here? she thought. *Still, they should be captured and pay for the terrible crime they had committed.*

"Are you able to tell us anything more about those men, Julie?" Joel asked.

"Oh, yes," she sighed. "I do remember. I do. It was terrible. I remember everything now." They all followed her into the living room and sat down by the comforting fire. Shaking her head and releasing a heavy sigh, Julie began her story.

"My father worked for the railroad. My family followed him in his travels, ending in the west. We settled just outside of Tacoma. Father ascertained that many Washington emigrants had traveled by trains before they left the east, and knew what a railroad could do for the western territory. Enthused, he encouraged everyone to join him in talking up railroads and the need for a Northern Pacific line to help link the country to-

74

gether. He felt possibly this would help stimulate the desire of including the Washington Territory as one of the United States. But, Father found the rails were slow in coming. Many people in the government back east could not be convinced that the far-off territory was really worth the trouble or expense.

"While waiting for a Northern Pacific line, some of the nearby towns pulled together what resources they could. They went ahead and laid tracks between scattered settlements, looking forward to the day their efforts might connect with the much longer lines. Father was one of the men who became instrumental in getting the Kalama-Tacoma rail line underway.

"In the meantime, to help provide housing and provisions for our family, Father worked in a nearby lumber mill. One night he got involved in a terrible fight, and was shot in the thigh. His leg became infected and had to be amputated. This brought about a distressing change in my father. He seemed to lose all the enthusiasm for life he formerly had, even with a wooden leg. I never learned the reason for the fight.

"Mother had been a city girl, never quite able to cope with the hardships and loneliness of the western life. She yearned for her close-knit family back in Indiana, and tried hard to keep it from Father. I found her many times in silent tears. I know Mama really wanted to be a good wife to the man she so dearly loved. But after he was left crippled, so much stress and more work was thrust upon her. Then she came down with 'the Fever' soon after Suelena, my older sister, left home to teach school near Olympia. I took care of Mama the best I could, along with the housework, some cooking, and such.

"A couple days after Mama became sick, Father hitched the horses to our wagon and sent me into town to buy some supplies. Upon my return I noticed a fire in the distance. At first I didn't think too much about it. Loggers many times would burn piles of brush in open spaces. But the closer I got to home, I realized it was our home in flames. I flapped the reins to speed up the team. I felt overcome with fear for my family. I became frantic.

"As I approached the house, I could see three men on horses inciting the fire. One of the men noticed me and yelled to the other two. They directed their mounts towards me. The big, grizzly man grabbed my arm and tried to pull me out of the wagon, as the three drew near the buckboard. Our neighbors happened to arrive at that moment with offers of help. The other two awful men saw them approaching and hollered at the grizzly man. Then all three rode off in the opposite direction yelling out their threats that they would get me, knowing I could identify them.

"I jumped off the wagon and found my father lying by the barn. He had been shot several times and was lying there dead. I tried to enter our home to help my mother out of the house," tears of grief flowed down Julie's cheeks by this time, "But the flames and heat were so intense. I coughed from so much smoke and tried again. The neighbors kept pulling me back from the roaring fire. I screamed that Mama was still inside. But they continued to restrain me, saying it was too late, that Mama would already be dead, that nobody could live through such extreme heat and smoke. I helped them throw buckets of well water on the flames. It did little good. The fire finally burned itself out. Our friends tried to persuade me to go home with them, but I just couldn't leave. They helped me bury Father, and then, exhausted, left to go to their respective homes, begging me to go with them." Julie was sobbing now.

"I slept in the barn that night. The next morning I searched through the ashes. All I could find was Mama's golden wedding band reflecting in the sun." She twisted the band of gold she wore on her finger. The long-awaited tears continued to fall as she cried, "I wanted to die. Why didn't I die, too? Everything is gone. My dear, sweet Mother, so fragile, always so thoughtful . . . loving . . . kind. My devoted father . . . our home and all our possessions he worked so hard to achieve for us. . . ."

"Suelena! I've got to find Suelena. She must not know what has happened," she cried out loud.

"Dear, dear Julie. You've been through so much. We'll get the sheriff to trace down your sister," Joel offered, as he held her in his fatherly arms. "Do you remember your family's name?"

"Our name is Dillon. My name is Valora Edith Dillon. My father named me after his mother, Valora, and my Aunt Edith, who live back in Indiana."

"That's a lovely name . . . Valora."

Six

Paul decided to travel with Sheriff Randal to help track down Valora's sister. It seemed strange to call Julie, Valora. However, the name had a rather pleasing sound. At least the girl hadn't changed and the band of gold symbolized a remembrance not a commitment.

Since the rain would not let up, making the roads and trails muddy and unpleasant to travel, the trek to Olympia took several days. Both men wore slickers made from animal hides, which helped them to stay warm and dry. Fall was slowly creeping in, bringing a chill to the evening air. Some of the leaves already were starting to turn hillsides from green to shades of browns, golds, oranges and reds.

After arriving in Olympia, they located the Sheriff's office and inquired about the young woman teacher. Relieved with the knowledge he knew of her, they learned that she most likely lived on the east side of town, probably in a boarding house close to the only school in the area. After finding the neat two-story structure, Sheriff Randal knocked on the door and found the young lady truly did reside there. Directions were given to locate her quarters upstairs; the second room on the right from the top of the stairs.

The two men ascended the stairs, found the room and knocked on the door. Immediately a tall slender woman with raven, black hair answered.

"Hello, ma'am. I'm Sheriff Randal and my friend is Paul

McCalister. We're looking for a Miss Suelena Dillon," the sheriff began.

"I'm Suelena. May I be of help to you?" She gave a hesitant, questioning smile. "Please, do come in."

"I'm afraid we have some painful news for you. You'd better sit down, Miss Dillon." Paul motioned to a nearby chair. "I've come with Sheriff Randal to bring you some sad news. I don't know how to break the tragic news to you gently. There was a fire. Your mother and father were both found dead."

Teardrops started to flow from the blue eyes of the young woman. After a moment she looked up pathetically at both men. Her hand clasped over her mouth trying to keep from crying out. In a controlled, but anguished voice she managed to ask, "What about my sister, Valora? Is she dead, too?" Her tear, stained face shone with deepest concern.

"Your sister appears fine now. She has been staying with my family in Cascadia. Until recently she could not remember any of the tragedy. The doctor told us she had amnesia. When she finally realized what had happened, she asked us to find you."

Paul suggested she sit down in a nearby chair and went on to recount the story that Valora had related to the McCalister family.

"I must go to my sister." The lovely lady rose from her chair.

"That's our reason for being here. You're welcome to ride back with us, if you like," the sheriff offered.

"I'll probably need a day or two to find someone to take my position at school. Can you wait that long?"

"We'll stay as long as necessary," they both agreed.

"You've been very kind to help my sister, and now me. Have you been able to locate the three men who did such a terrible thing?"

"We're still in the process of trying to locate them. You can be assured we won't quit searching until we bring the scoundrels to justice," the sheriff confirmed.

After the men left her room, Suelena collapsed on the bed releasing her suppressed emotions. Leaving her family had been very difficult, knowing how hard it was on her mother to say good-bye. Still, Suelena knew her parents understood the excitement she had felt about the teaching position she had procured. Through their encouragement she had accepted the placement, since Olympia wasn't too far from home. She often wondered why her letters the last few months had gone unanswered. Sometimes she felt so lonely she would come to the conclusion that maybe they didn't feel her absence as much as she missed them; then at times she reasoned they must have been too busy with the farm.

Suelena had wanted so badly to go home during the summer months, but her finances just didn't allow that luxury. A teacher didn't earn a very large salary. Father had brought her to Olympia on the buckboard to begin her teaching career. Horses were not all that plentiful, and even if she could find one to purchase, she had never learned to ride one.

Now the new school year was about to begin. The job at the little café in town, working as a part-time cook and waitress, had helped to pay her expenses during the summer months. But her real joy remained teaching. She found it very rewarding to be a part of helping children grow in knowledge.

Mrs. Wright . . . maybe she'll fill in for me for a few weeks. Although she's retired from teaching, she's always telling me how she misses the youngsters, Suelena thought, finally dozing off to a restless sleep.

Time dragged by until dawn's light peeked through the lace curtains. Bright and early the young woman started to pack her clothes with mixed emotions about the journey. She, of course, was anxious to see her younger sister, but the trip . . . that presented another matter.

She went to see Mrs. Wright right after finishing her packing. Her friend seemed rather pleased to accept the teaching position. "You go on and enjoy visiting with your sister." She had been very understanding and expressed her sorrow over the loss of Suelena's parents. "But do remember my substituting is only for a few weeks. I am retired, you know." She presented a stern face that shortly turned into a compassionate smile.

The next concern on Suelena's agenda was to see the blacksmith about purchasing a horse. "One that is very tame and slow," she pleaded with the man.

Pausing for a moment, he chuckled, and then finally said he had just the right animal for her. The husky man went to the stables and led out a bay with a medium, brown body, black mane and tail, with a white blaze on his forehead. His back seemed to be shaped rather funny; but the blacksmith only wanted twenty-five dollars. Satisfied with the price, she paid him the money and led the horse by the reins in the direction of the boarding house somewhat pleased with herself. Upon arriving at the residence she found the sheriff and Paul waiting on the porch for her return.

"Whatcha got there, Mr. Swayback?" Paul yelled out snickering.

"He's my new horse. I've named him Blaze." Suelena answered. "Don't you just love him? I find him quite sweet, and he's supposed to be gentle."

"Where's his saddle?" the sheriff asked.

"Saddle? Uh, I forgot a saddle. Oh, well, I'll ride him without one."

They both looked at each other and grinned. "Okay. I hope you know what you're doing," Paul went on. "I sure hope you can ride better than your sister did." He winked at the sheriff.

She wasn't about to let them know her knowledge of horses happened to be very slight. If truth be told, she felt sure she had never even been on one.

"Were you able to find someone to teach while you're away?" the sheriff asked.

"Yes, thank you. Also, I've quit my job at the café and I'm ready anytime you two would like to leave."

"Fine. Let's get started now. We've a long trip ahead of us. We'll ride as far as we can before we set up camp tonight," Paul suggested.

"I'll get my things." She tied the horse to a post, then went inside the boarding house and on up the stairs; the two men trailing not far behind.

One of the men grabbed the luggage bag from off the bed. Suelena reached for her pillow and blanket.

"Is that all?" Paul asked relieved. "You're traveling light."

"No. There's two more bags in the closet."

"Two more!" the sheriff groaned. "You're only going to be gone a few days!"

"But that's all I own. I have no other place to keep my things, since I'm giving up the room to save on expenses. The owner told me I shouldn't have any trouble getting another room when I return."

"Yeh. All right, we'll each have to carry a bag on our horse, unless you have a buggy, too." His eyes rolled around, as he picked up a bag and moved toward the stairs.

Now, how do I get on this animal? she thought, then decided to move the horse up to the porch. She placed the blanket on his back, the pillow on top and proceeded to climb onto the animal. Just then the horse decided to move and Suelena, the blanket and pillow fell to the ground.

Paul, being the closest to her, went to the young lady's

aid. "Would you care for some help?" He tried extremely hard to conceal a grin, as he rubbed his hand over his mouth and reached out his other hand to help her up. Her hair had fallen in disarray from the bun she had pinned on the top of her head. The long, light, brown skirt bounded up over her bosom, showing several layers of petticoats. Then she attempted to get up and straighten her clothing at the same time. All the while she tried to make an earnest attempt at being dignified, not wanting to show the terrible embarrassment she felt inside.

"Miss Suelena, if I may, I would like to suggest we stop by the general store and see about purchasing a saddle. I'm sure you would be much more . . . ah, satisfied. We have a long journey ahead of us," the sheriff recommended with a touch of consternation in his voice.

"I would like to, sir, but I don't think I have enough money." She was not going to release those mortified tears.

"I'll loan you the money. You can pay me back whenever . . ." Paul urged without hesitation.

The general store had a good used saddle at a fair price, so Suelena accepted the offer. With the help of the men, the horse was saddled, Suelena helped on his back, the blanket, pillow and bag strapped on. The three finally started on their journey with Suelena holding on to the reins, as well as grasping the horn of the saddle, trying hard to hide her fear.

After starting their trip, the weather grew cloudy and overcast; soon it started to drizzle . . . again. Suelena wrapped her warm, brown, leather jacket tighter around her body. She wondered how in the world the men could ride so smooth in their saddles, while all she could do is go bump, bump, bounce, bounce, sliding from side to side, as her horse galloped on and on.

Finally, Sheriff Randal hollered, "Try pressing your knees

in to the body of the horse, press your feet down in the stir-rups, and fall in rhythm with the horse."

She tried. She really did. But the dear girl just couldn't seem to get the hang of it. As she was coming down, the horse was going up. In truth, she felt so miserable wondering if the time would ever come to set up camp for the night. Still, not wanting to complain, she determined that would be the last thing those men would hear from her.

The gray clouds suspended in the mist grew darker and the stormy wind began to summon in stronger blustery gusts. She really had to work at staying warm, while wishing she had remembered to keep out a pair of warm gloves. Soon the clouds seemed to burst apart with the rain turning into a steady downpour. Could there have been a worse day to travel? She didn't think do.

I must think about seeing Valora, she thought. *It will be so good to see family again.* Her mind wandered back to happier days, when they were little girls. Even then, Suelena loved to play school; always wanting to be the teacher for her younger sister, reading her stories and teaching her how to read and spell some of the words. They had moved so often because of their father's travels with the railroad, that they didn't have an opportunity to make many close friends, and when they did they would cry when they had to leave them for another move. So they became each other's best friend.

Valora took after her mother's side of the family. She was petite and lovely with her red hair and dark, brown eyes. Suelena favored her father's ancestors, with fair skin, blue eyes, tall in stature and dark hair. They looked enough like sisters and yet so different. What family they had left made their home back in Indiana as far as she knew.

Just then a clap of thunder roared and lightning lit up the heavens. Her horse spooked, bounding forward, passing her companions as the panic struck animal ran fiercely, uncontrolled. Suelena didn't know what to do except hold on as tight to the saddle horn as she could.

Finally, Blaze came to a stop alongside a rushing stream. She struggled to climb down from the saddle. Her legs felt like scrambled eggs. At that moment Paul jumped off his horse and grabbed her. The young woman's frightened face, drained of color, looked up into his. Her body couldn't stop trembling, and then she collapsed into his arms.

A crackling sound could be heard coming from a warm campfire, when Suelena opened her eyes. The well blackened pot of steaming coffee hung over an open fire. Sheriff Randal stood nearby stirring a pot of stew, sending off a delightful aroma, tantalizing her taste buds, which gnawed at her empty stomach.

Her body felt as if every muscle and joint had changed places, as the young woman started to get up from the pallet that had been prepared for her under a makeshift shelter. "Something sure smells delicious over there," she tried to sound cheerful. "I could eat a horse!" A giggle let out from her mouth. "And maybe I will before this trip is over." The men both chuckled.

"It's been quite a day. Are you feeling better now?" Sheriff Randal asked concerned.

"I'll be fine," she grinned, "once I learn how to handle that horse."

"You really did quite well. I didn't think you'd stay on Blaze when the lightning frightened him," Paul said. "You should have warned us that you're not a horseback rider."

"It was that obvious?" She wrinkled her nose.

"I'm afraid so, ma'am." They both laughed.

The warmth of the campfire and the tasty food gave her more determination than ever to not be a problem to these two men. She didn't know why, but Suelena felt comfortable around them. Usually she became very shy and restrained in the presence of the opposite sex. But Paul and the sheriff seemed different. Both had been very kind and showed concern for her. She liked them, and hoped she wouldn't do any more dumb things to cause them to dislike her.

It rained all night. The men had taken turns stoking the fire and keeping watch, as the howling of wolves could be heard in the distance. At daybreak each one woke up, wishing for a relief from the inclement weather. The gushing creek even appeared fuller than it had yesterday.

"Let's get going as soon as possible. Maybe we can reach Cascadia tomorrow," the sheriff said, offering Suelena a tin cup of steaming coffee, which she received with an appreciative smile.

"Just to have a roof over our heads and a soft bed again would be a nice change . . . not that I don't appreciate the sleeping quarters you fixed for me last night," she added quickly.

"We understand. Home and being with family is always the best place to be. Still, it is good to get out in the wild like this once in a while, so we can recognize its worth and value our homes and families," Paul replied.

The bedrolls and cooking utensils were securely packed on the horses' backs. Suelena's body felt so stiff and sore; she thought she'd never be able to straighten out her bowed legs ever again. This time Sheriff Randal offered to help her into the saddle, which she dreaded. But, knowing the horse as being the only mode of transportation available, and yearning to see her sister, she gladly accepted his kind gesture.

Even though rain still kept falling, the unique scenery remained magnetic. A pleasant, fresh, woodsy aroma filled the air. Birds sat perched in the trees chirping along the trail with squirrels chattering back at them. A small quiet lake stood out like a jewel as it sparkled across a lush, green meadow. How could you not be aware of the beauty God had fashioned for His creation to enjoy?

The three anxious people rode side by side when they could, each preoccupied in their own thoughts. By afternoon the sun tried to wedge its way through the weeping clouds. The rain gradually turned into showers. After a while they came upon a river needing to be crossed; it didn't seem to bother the men's horses, probably because the men shown no fear, and in obvious control. But poor Blaze, he had no intention of entering the swift, flowing water; and he surely must have sensed that his female companion didn't feel too keen about the idea either. Nothing she knew to do would coax the frightened animal into the cold rushing river.

Paul finally took the reins of the bay and led him into the icy water. Again, Suelena became convinced the saddle horn had been designed just for occasions like this, as she clasped both hands tightly to this prized possession. Many times on this trip she learned to be thankful for the men to have encouraged her into buying the saddle instead of riding bareback. She knew by now she would never have come this far without the protection of the seat. In fact, the more she pondered the idea, and even knowing she would be teased, sitting on a pillow sounded mighty tempting under the present circumstances.

At last they stumbled to the other side of the rapidly moving river, not quite sure which one appeared more grateful . . . Paul . . . Suelena . . . or the horse.

"Let's take a break here," Paul suggested.

"No argument from me," came Suelena's hurried reply.

Sheriff Randal set up a campfire to warm his companions and started up the old faithful coffee pot. Soon the hot beverage helped melt away the chill from the cold.

"How much farther do we have to travel?" Suelena asked, not directing the question to either men, more for conversation.

"We should make our destination by tomorrow evening, Ma'am," the sheriff answered.

"I surely hope so. I knew the trip would be rough traveling, but I will be glad to get there . . . so I can see Valora again," she added quickly.

Although a little earlier than they had planned to make camp, each one agreed they might as well stay in this place for tonight. The tired horses needed rest along with their equally weary riders.

Valiant, evergreen trees stretched toward the muted sky. Foothills of the centuries old Cascades could be seen across the fast flowing river. Mt. Rainier soared majestically higher than its sister peaks in all its splendor, while standing sentinel over the surrounding area like a king over his court. Nothing stood in the way to obscure the captivating view. A refreshing breeze dashed across Suelena's unblemished face, gracefully blowing her long hair that was released from the tight bun she had been wearing. She felt as if captured in a charm of spiritual loveliness.

She turned her head and found Paul gazing at her with a pleasing impression on his wholesome face. A smile crossed his lips. For some reason she felt embarrassed, as she stared into his eyes for only a moment, then quickly turned away. She wondered if this handsome man was married. Surely he must have a multitude of young women contending for his attention, if not.

Suddenly Sheriff Randal placed his towering body beside her. "You unmistakably have the same possession of such qualities that delight the eye as your sister."

"Huh, uh, oh. I do enjoy God's beauty," she stammered. "Don't you?"

"You bet. I admire the scenery, a fine faithful horse, and the pleasant company of a good friend, and an impressive woman," he said with a grin.

Seven

The rain had finally subsided. Valora felt a fresh serene feeling permeating the air. Some of the autumn leaves gently began to fall from the colorful trees, covering the pathway to the barn. She still enjoyed the trips to the Judsons' homestead each morning to feed the chickens in the early opal dawn. Now and then Mr. Judson allowed her to milk one of the cows just to keep up the practice; but Valora knew she would never win a contest for speed. She had grown to love this quiet, gentle man and the feeling was mutual.

"When is your sister coming?" he asked. Conversation between the two flowed easily nowadays.

"Any day now, sir. I can hardly wait. It seems like Paul and the sheriff have been gone a month. I hope they aren't having trouble locating her." She stopped what she was doing to ponder on those words.

"I know the McCalisters have treated you fine. Still, I'm sure it will be such a sweet consolation having a beloved relative to share memories with." She could tell he still missed his dear wife, Emma.

"They certainly have been wonderful to me. I couldn't ask for any kinder people. Papa Mack treats me as if I were his daughter. Yes, I am excited about seeing my sister. We've always been very close. I know she'll love you, Sarah and your family as I do."

After a few minutes Valora completed her job. "I'd better be going on home. I want to have breakfast ready for my hungry men, when they come in from their chores. I'll see you to-morrow, Mr. Judson." She smiled and waved good-bye.

"Take some fresh eggs with you," he called out to her.

"Much obliged."

Valora rode her sorrel back to the ranch. First, she stopped at the pen housing the little bear cubs. "My, you've grown. You're going to eat us out of our welcome one of these days," she laughed. They growled back at her, as if giving her an answer in return.

"Yes, Gruffy, I brought you something to eat, and you too, Big Nose. You bears sure live up to your names. Now, just wait your turn." They started to sniff in her pockets for more. "That's all now. I'll see you later. I have work to do."

When the men came in the dining room, Valora had breakfast ready for serving. "Good morning, Jul . . . mmm, sorry. I still have trouble calling you Valora, even if it is a pretty name," Papa Mack apologized. "Everything sure smells luscious. I see you've made some blackberry jelly. We'll have to try some on those great-looking biscuits."

"Biscuits and jelly. That sounds mighty tempting," Tom agreed. "You're becoming a real fine cook, Valora."

"She'll make someone a delightful wife," Papa Mack winked. "Pretty too."

Both Valora and Tom turned a blushing red. She had already surmised that Tom was not the marrying kind; although a very likeable person with a pleasing personality and ruggedly handsome good looks, he seemed to enjoy keeping to himself. His father depended on him a great deal in running the ranch. Tom held the responsibility of the buying and selling of their cattle and horses, and also was in charge of the ranch hands. The men appeared to have a good rapport with him; she couldn't help but notice how they honored him with highest regard.

Paul enjoyed the detail part and took pleasure in learning

the responsibility of keeping the books. Mark revered the homestead, but felt his calling was in the medical world. A close-knit family, they unmistakenly found satisfaction in one another's company. Evenings became a time of exchanging their thoughts of the happenings of the day. Valora delighted in sitting back listening to their dialogue, pleased they allowed her to join them. However, she didn't very often add much to their conversation on ranching, except when it came to the house. Sometimes the men didn't agree with one another, but they respected each other's opinions, rarely arguing.

Joel went into town early the next morning, wanting to question the bartender of the tavern about the three varmints. He learned that yesterday had been their first appearance in the saloon. They were rather raucous characters, trying to pick a fight with whoever would accept the challenge, mostly the other customers just ignored them. However, they did brag they would be back.

"Did you learn their names or where they might be going?" Joel probed the bartender.

"Said they were camped outside of town. Wanted to know if I'd seen a red-haired girl around these parts, that they had some business with her. I had heard about the girl you have staying at your ranch, but I didn't give out any information about her," he assured Joel.

"Thanks, Dobbs. You've been a great help. And please, keep quiet about Valora. I hope we can detain them from leaving the area until Sheriff Randal returns. We're sure they are the culprits we've been looking for."

While Joel rode into town, Valora went about her regular duties in the home. She had grown fond of the impressive log house, knowing that much of the imposing but comfortable furniture Joel had crafted with his own masterful skill. Lace curtains graced the windows and crocheted doilies decorated the tables, she supposed Mattie had sewn. A good-sized, well equipped kitchen opened up into the family's dining room. Along one wall of the expansive living area shelves supported numerous books and sentimental collections. A solid structure of gray stone enclosing the fireplace occupied another wall. An enormous roll top desk filled a large part of the third wall.

Three sizable bedrooms claimed the second floor, each opening to a full length balcony which overlooked the living area below. The guest room that Valora utilized and Joel's master bedroom were on the ground floor. A covered porch took possession of the front of the dwelling, where a swing hung suspended from the ceiling, and well-used rocking chairs commanded much of the rest of the covered portico.

A disturbance outside quickly interrupted Valora from her pleasant meditations. *Oh, dear,* she thought, *those mischievous bears are at it again!* She decided she'd better investigate. Grabbing her jacket she ran towards their pen. Just as she opened the gate someone grabbed her from behind, clasping his grubby, smelly hand over her mouth to subdue a scream. Then very roughly he dragged her into the barn nearby, all the while she kicked and tried in desperation to get away.

To her horror, inside were the other two men she had seen in town the day before. The heavy scar-faced man had a sinister grin on his bushy face, showing grimy-stained teeth. She remembered Tom saying earlier that he and the ranch hands needed to do some more checking of the fences today, because of some strays wandering about and for her to please stay inside the house; with Joel in town that left her alone. Panic filled her emotions.

Finally, the man released his grip over her mouth. "Ho . . . how did you find me?" she couldn't believe the words came out, as she looked toward the leader of the pack.

"It wasn't hard. I bribed a drunk in the saloon in town yesterday. He told me a red-haired girl was staying at the McCalister ranch and gave us directions here. When we left the saloon, I thought for sure I saw you coming out of the store across the street. We pretended to leave in the opposite direction, but followed you at a distance, since you had a man riding alongside the wagon. When he started to turn around, we hid in the trees. Then we decided to make camp in the woods not far from the ranch and waited till it became clear. The men made it easy by leaving you alone today. We saw them ride out not long ago." He let loose a nauseous laugh.

"Why did you kill my parents?" Valora nearly screamed with anger.

"Your father fired me from my job on the railroad." His mouth developed into an ugly smirk.

"So you killed him? It had to be more than that!" She became more furious.

"Yeh, your father caught me stealing several times. I shot him in the leg the last time, the no good bum. Enough talk. I wouldn't be telling you all this, but it's now your time to die," His grimy teeth began to show. "I can't have anyone left to identify me, can I?" He let out a wicked laugh.

"Not if I have anything to do with it. Drop your gun or I'll blow your head off!" Tom had ridden back to the ranch unnoticed. Knowing his father had gone into town earlier, he didn't want to leave Valora alone. When he couldn't find the girl in the house, worried, he started looking for her. Overhearing unfamiliar, obtrusive voices coming from the barn, he crept around to the back and quietly approached the burly man from behind. "Drop it, I said," as he jammed the nose of the rifle in the intruder's neck and cocked the trigger.

Just then a fierce snarl came from the entry released by two angry animals walking on their hind legs. Gruffy caught one of the men by the throat, killing him instantly. The man grasping Valora threw her to the ground and shot at the enraged animal, wounding it. The other bear attacked him. His gun went off. Both man and bear fell instantly to the ground.

93

A struggle arose between Tom and his captive. First, one would strike the face of his opponent, then the other would connect. Valora watched helplessly. Each man was slamming his opposer all over the barn, only to get up, and forge on once more. During the conflict, Tom dropped his weapon. Valora picked it up; the cocked rifle somehow discharged in Valora's hand. The terrifying ordeal suddenly came to a halt.

Valora ran over to where Tom lay still on the straw-covered floor. "Tom! Tom!" she cried out. His face was covered with blood; his clothes nearly torn from his battered body. Tears streamed down her cheeks. "Oh, Tom, please be all right." She dropped to the floor beside him and raised his head, picking it up to her bosom, kissing his face and hugging it gently in her arms while rocking back and forth begging him to be all right. Slowly he opened one eye and then the other. Looking up into her eyes, a smile gradually spread across his face.

"Are you all right?" she whispered. "I was so frightened. I dropped the rifle. It went off. I thought I'd killed you. Oh, Tom, you've always been here when I've needed you. How did you know where to find me?" She started kissing all over his face again . . . and then . . . he returned her kiss. Suddenly they both realized what was happening.

"Valora. My dear, beautiful, Valora." Tom cupped her face in his strong, gentle hands and said, "I think I've been in love with you ever since that day you tried to mount the horse on the wrong side and fell off." He smiled. "But you were wearing that band of gold, and it appeared you belonged to another man. Then Paul started to care about you, so I backed off."

"You've always been so nice to me, but I really didn't think you cared in that way." She paused to look at his handsome face. "I, I think I'm in love with you, too." Her caressing eyes captured his. He gently smoothed the back of his hand over her cheek and brushed a strand of hair from her eyes. Then his lips touched hers again, so tenderly. Valora never had sensations radiate through her body like she was feeling now. It almost frightened her.

"This moment is a gift. I've wanted to embrace you in my arms for so long," he whispered and kissed her once again.

They heard a whimper across the barn, reawakening the terrifying situation they had just encountered. "It's Gruffy. He's alive!" Valora ran over to her pet. "Oh, he's bleeding. But it's only his leg. We can fix that up, can't we?" She looked pleadingly at Tom.

"We'll sure give it a try."

"Poor little Big Nose. They both helped save my life, along with you, Tom. But one of our little heroes is dead." Then she saw the three men lying across the barn lifeless, and the tears began to well up and flow down her cheeks again. What a dreadful day. Will the visions of this day allow a peaceful solitude to ever be restored any time soon?

Joel appeared at the entrance to the barn. "What in tarnation happened here?" His face saturated with alarm as he glanced quickly around the barn. "Valora! Tom! Are you all right?" Then the couple related the terrible experience.

"I'll get the hands to load up the men's bodies and take them into town for burial. You both go on in the house and get cleaned up." He couldn't help but notice the tattered appearance of his son. "You've been through enough for a lifetime." The father shook his head in disbelief. "I'm so sorry I wasn't here."

"It's over, Papa Mack. Tom was my hero, and so were the bears."

"I'll fix up Gruffy. He'll be as good as new real soon. I'll also take care of his companion." He shook his head again with an incredulous relief.

Eight

The three travelers were anxious to get moving, as the glow of sunrise gradually spread its colorful tones over the surrounding mountains. Mt. Rainier stood exquisitely clothed in shades of peach with silver, outlining the puffy, pink clouds high above. The crisp air felt invigorating, encouraging them the desire to hurry their camping chores along. Suelena had glorious expectations for the day. She found walking not quite as painful as yesterday. "Maybe I'll get adept to riding a horse yet," she hoped silently.

"We'll have to ride at a faster pace today, if we plan to reach Cascadia by nightfall," Paul asserted.

Suelena gulped. "I'll do my best not to be a hindrance." She relied more on the reins than the saddle horn now. Still glad to find it there just in case.

The overgrown trail proved even more rugged than yesterday, as it led up one rolling hill and then another. She had given up wearing her hair in a bun and found braids much easier to keep her long, dark locks under control. The branches of trees and bushes slapped her in the face, causing the tresses to look unkept. She wasn't too fond of this; being neat tended to be more her characteristic.

At a distance they spied a herd of elk grazing in the inviting golden meadow by a transparent stream. The stalwart leader of the herd glanced with curiosity toward the riders seemingly undisturbed by their presence. That created pleasure for Suelena, because she certainly had no desire to harm them and was glad the wild animals perceived that sense.

They came upon a waterfall hearing the resounding roar afar off. "How spectacular!" she exclaimed. "I'd sure like to get a drink of some fresh water, if you don't mind."

"We can stop and have lunch, if you'd like. We still have fish and biscuits left from breakfast," the sheriff suggested.

She wrinkled her nose a little, then expressed, "This setting makes anything taste good." They ate their snack in silence, then the young woman spoke, "I was hungrier than I thought. I see we still have some leftovers. It reminds me of the little boy in the Bible who offered his five loaves of bread and two fish to Jesus. After He thanked God and blessed it, a multitude of people ate, and His disciples gathered up twelve baskets of leftovers." (John 6:8–13)

"You read the Bible, too?" Paul asked with an expression of surprised pleasure.

"Yes. Mama always encouraged us to read and memorize scripture. She had a deep faith in our Lord and wanted her children to have a personal faith in Him also. I don't know what I would have done many times, when I felt so lonely, if it hadn't been knowing I had a friend watching out for and reassuring me . . . even me." She gazed up into Paul's face. "Do you understand what I am saying, Paul?"

"Yes, I do. When my mother died, my faith in God carried me through the rough times, and of course my family."

"You lost your mother, too?" She looked astonished.

"She went to be with the Lord the early part of this year. In fact, we had just buried Mother the day your sister found our ranch and we took her in."

They both leaned back against a fallen log, absorbed in the solitude of the moment. Then the less interested Sheriff Randal broke the silence. "We better get moving on. We've still a long trail before us."

97

The sun shone bright high overhead with the warmth of its rays filtering through the trees, arousing agreeable feelings. "Looks like we might have an 'Indian Summer' this year after all." Paul smiled, reinforcing his pleasant thoughts. "I enjoy it when summer takes its time to roll over into fall." He mounted his buckskin horse, after helping Suelena on to her steed.

After a while the trail led along a hillside with protruding boulders and tall trees, when all of a sudden a ferocious growl startled the trio. From out of nowhere a fierce animal sprang, knocking Suelena from her mount. She hit the rocky earth with a thud. She screamed as the monstrous wildcat vaulted toward her. Instantly, Paul bounded off his horse, while grabbing his hunting knife from his leather belt. With his strong arms he pulled the cougar away from the terrified girl and wrestled with the ornery animal, stabbing it several times with the sharp weapon. Suelena couldn't control the trembling caused from insurmountable fear. But wanting to help Paul in some way, she grabbed on to the vicious animal's tail, trying desperately to pull it away from the one who was risking his life for hers. The startled cat instinctively turned his attention back in her direction just long enough for the sheriff to get a perfect aim. He fired his rifle immediately into the animal's body. In only a matter of minutes the dramatic confrontation ended. The mountain lion fell dead beside his battered opponent.

"Paul! Paul! Are you all right?" Suelena managed to crawl over to him. Her blouse had been ripped open in several places, showing numerous scratches. Paul lay silent, motionless on the cold ground. He had a deep gash in his side and his battered arms bled through his tattered shirt.

"Is he dead?" Her huge eyes stared up into Randal's face with sympathetic tears sliding down her injured face.

The sheriff checked his friend for a pulse. "He's alive. But we've got to get him to a doctor. We've got to try to stop the bleeding first."

Suelena pulled off the clothing bag from her horse and found one of her petticoats and ripped it into large strips. With some water from a canteen, she managed to wipe some of the blood from his arms and face to clean and disclose the depth of the wounds. She then wrapped the clean cloths around his side. One arm appeared to be even worse than the side, so she wrapped the arm and made him a sling.

All the while the sheriff set out to frame a travois out of tree limbs, covering it with a blanket, then fastened the rig onto Paul's horse so he could travel. "I believe I remember seeing a farmhouse a mile or so back. We'd better take him there till I can locate a doctor. It's a good thing he's unconscious. The journey will be hard on him in such condition."

Traveling proved very slow. It probably took a couple hours before catching sight of the dilapidated old farmhouse. As they drew near a big brutish looking man holding a shotgun come out of the house along with two small, ragged children. He pushed them back inside the house.

"What da ya want?" His voice sounded unfriendly.

"I'm Sheriff Randal. We've got an injured man here, and wondered how far it is to a doctor."

"Ha!" the man grunted. "There ain't no doc around here fer miles."

Just then a scrawny, plain woman came out the door. "Bring him in here. I can help."

"Shut yer mouth, woman. They ain't talkin' to you."

"This man is badly hurt, sir. I'd be mighty obliged to you, if you'd let your wife help." The sheriff pushed his way inside. The house really didn't appear as dirty as he thought it would be, to his relief.

"I served as a nurse before I married my husband," the woman spoke softly.

The sheriff looked astonished, then smiled. "We'd appreciate your help, ma'am."

"Buck, please help them bring the injured man in." She motioned to the disgruntled man."

"Oh, all right," he growled.

The two men carried Paul to a bed under the instructions of the sheriff. Nothing about the other man expressed gentleness. Quickly the woman removed the blood-stained cloths and asked Suelena to get some hot water from the teapot on the pot-bellied stove and pour it into a clean bucket sitting beside the cupboard. She cleaned him up with skillful hands, applying a strong-smelling poultice onto his wounds and dressed them with clean cloths.

"This will help keep down the infection and loss of blood until you can get him to a doctor. He really shouldn't travel. Please stay here for the night. What he needs now is some rest." Her voice was gentle and showed concern.

"You're so kind. If it's all right with your husband, we'd like to stay." Suelena had been watching her competent hands. "May I help in any way?"

"You'd better let me look at your injuries, ma'am."

Suelena had forgotten about herself. She did look a mess. Her hair fell in disarray and her blouse had been badly torn in shreds. Bonnie checked cuts and scratches; none appeared as deep as Paul's wounds. But they did need to be cleaned. She applied the medication and carefully bandaged them.

"Let's get supper started. If you feel up to it, you may help with that." She smiled with a hint of sadness in her expression.

Suelena assisted by peeling potatoes and carrots for a stew. While the older woman skinned the rabbit her companion had brought in, Suelena tried to make conversation. "My name is Suelena Dillon. The injured man is Paul McCalister. You've already met Sheriff Randal."

She found the children eager for her attention. "My name's Charlie," the little boy grinned. Although his clothes were patched and too small, they were clean.

"My name is Evalene." The blond-haired girl didn't want to be left out. "My Mommy calls me Evie."

"That's such a pretty name. How old are you, Evie?"

"I'm this many." She held up four fingers.

"I'm six," said Charlie, as his clear, blue eyes gleamed.

"That's enough now. You two go on and play while Miss Suelena and I finish up supper." The mother smiled lovingly at her children. Even though she looked very thin and her deep sunken eyes had that heavy-heartedness about them, Suelena decided that some personal care—and if her straggly light brown hair was fashioned in a becoming style—she could be a very attractive woman.

The stew and cornbread tasted wonderful. After camping out for several days, sitting and eating at a table provided a real treat. Conversation remained limited though during the meal. The children seemed afraid of doing something wrong along with their mother, Bonnie. She had shared her name with her guest. The man of the family continued at being exceedingly gruff with table manners to match his obstinate disposition. Suelena wondered why such a sweet, well-educated woman would marry a man like Buck.

At bedtime Bonnie apologized for not having beds for her lodgers. Paul lay resting in one of the children's cots, and there was only one other bed.

"You'll have to sleep in the barn," said Buck. He had a smug smile on his face when he made the remark.

The sheriff answered with appreciation, as if untouched by his demeanor, "That will be fine. We have our own bedding."

Suelena decided to stay near Paul in case he started to wake up. She made herself a pallet on the floor beside his bed.

The children both slept on the other cot in the tiny room of the small house. Loud arguing could be heard from the nearby bedroom. She assumed the discussion probably included their visitors. Then, she heard someone fall to the floor. It turned into a fretful night.

When the early morning light began to radiate through the window, she heard Paul stirring from his bed. "Where am I?" His eyes finally settled on Suelena.

"Oh, Paul. I'm so glad you finally woke up. I've . . . we've been so worried about you," Suelena whispered. "I've been lying here praying and asking God to make you well. Do you remember the cougar attacking us? He bit and clawed you viciously in several places. The sheriff remembered seeing this farmhouse, so we brought you here. Bonnie, the lady of the house, cleaned and patched you up."

"I am awful sore, but I guess I'll live." He tried to smile although it hurt.

There was a knock at the door, then Bonnie came in the room. "How's my patient this morning?" She sounded almost cheerful.

"I think I look better than you. Where did you get that blackened face?" Paul couldn't help but ask.

"I fell out of bed last night." She turned away quickly. "I'll get you some breakfast."

"Sounds great. I'm starved."

"I'm sure he beats her. And she's so nice. Why does she put up with a louse like that?" Suelena whispered and shook her head in disgust after Bonnie had left the room. "I wish I could talk to her alone."

Soon biscuits and gravy were served. After the meal the women cleaned up the kitchen area, while the sheriff saddled the horses. The injured Paul decided he would rather try riding in the saddle than in the travois. If all went well they would be home by evening. Bonnie had checked his injuries and re-

102

dressed the wounds with the salve and clean cloths, encouraging him to see a doctor as soon as he could.

After expressing their gratitude and Suelena hugged the little ones good-bye, the party of three departed. Not far down the trail Suelena reached in her pocket to warm her hands from the early morning cold. It was then she discovered a folded piece of paper in one of her pockets of her coat. She took the paper out, unfolded it and discovered it was a note that read:

Dear Suelena:

Please help us. The man, Buck, living here is not my husband. He killed my Joshua several months ago and took over the farm and has made me and the children his prisoners. If you can help us, I would be forever grateful.

Sincerely,
Bonnie

She directed her horse over to Sheriff Randal an showed the note to him. "We've got to do something to get her away from that awful man," she pleaded with her eyes as well as her heart.

"Don't mention this to Paul. Let's get him home first. Meanwhile, I'll try to come up with some sort of a plan," the sheriff said.

The ride proceeded slowly. They had to stop several times for Paul to rest. He felt very weak and pale from the loss of blood. But, he was young and other than his wounds he received, was in good physical shape and wanting eagerly to improve. Bonnie's excellent nursing skills had proven her worthy of her title.

The weather grew kind for which they found pleasure. The sun's yellow rays glimmered through the dark clouds chasing away the rain, leaving just a few clouds in the bright blue sky. Robins were hunting for worms, while blue jays swooped down to aggravate them. Squirrels sat chattering in the trees as if they were scolding the pesky but beautiful black and brilliant, blue birds, telling them to fly away.

Darkness began to creep its way in by the time Paul caught a glimpse in the distance of the ranch he called home. "What a welcome sight. I've always enjoyed our home, but its appearance has never been more inviting." Relief showed in his haggard face.

The truth remaining, Suelena started to feel betrayed from mixed emotions. Some kindled a stimulating excitement and yet some fell susceptible to fear. The anxious longing to see her sister again, under the circumstances for which she had come, encouraged a deeply rooted emotion and delicate sentiment. Her thoughts of meeting the McCalister family induced an uneasiness within her. If the rest of the family turned out as kind and gentle as Paul, everything would be fine. Still, would they accept her as they had Valora? For her sister's sake she needed to be strong. All they had now would be each other and she was the oldest. All of these thoughts proceeded to churn around and plague her mind as well as her stomach.

Nine

An emotion of release spread through the McCalister household the next evening following the terrible ordeal with the three intruders. Just knowing the men who had taken the lives of Valora's parents in such a violent manner and had met their own death in an equally horrific ordeal didn't really bring the relief. But realizing she would not have to be concerned about them anymore and knowing they had received their just reward, however tragic, became the releasing factor.

"How unfortunate when hate and revenge are allowed to take over a person's mind. Why can't people seek the knowledge of forgiveness for one another and endeavor to live in harmony? We all make mistakes, but we need to learn from them and go on with our lives, accepting the responsibility of our own actions instead of blaming others. Sometimes we just need to look in a mirror and see who is really staring back at us." These were some of the thoughts that surged through Valora's mind as she sat rocking quietly on the front porch of this beloved dwelling she had so easily learned to call home. The days were growing shorter, introducing a chilling bite to the air. A shawl felt good. A slight breeze brought with it a reviving freshness.

Tom came out of the house and sat in the rocker beside her. He took her hand in his. "And what might my dear one be concerning yourself with? Are you still upset over the frightening episode of yesterday?"

"I'm fine. It's just been such an eventful year. I feel I've brought you and your family so much distress. I'm so sorry you have to become involved in my troubles."

"Valora, I believe God put us on earth to be of help to one another, when we can. We're not promised an easy existence. Life does have its problems. Sometimes we cause our own by our attitudes and selfishness, like those men. But it we own up to our mistakes, we can do something about them. It's much like becoming a Christian. First, you have to realize that you're not living a pleasing life. Then we need to feel sorry enough to ask God to forgive us of our sin, and ask Him to help us to live a better way.

"Sin isn't always murder, or stealing, or the so-called 'bad' things. We can hurt people with our tongue, as well as our actions. It's also lying, cheating, or failing to live up to one's potential. Unfortunately, some people never seem to learn that.

"I am thankful I happened along when you needed help. Valora, I always want to be here for you." His deep blue eyes scanned her lovely features.

She looked into his precious face, so filled with love and tenderness. "My dear, sweet Tom. I love you so very much," and their lips touched. A chill ran through her body.

The squeaking of the screen door opening, and a . . . "Ah, ha! We have two love birds out here! Now when did all this happen?" Joel had an approving grin on his face and a twinkle in his equally blue eyes.

Tom's impressive iron physique stood inches taller than his father, but right now his countenance quickly turned a handsome reddish tone. He cleared his throat. A high pitched, "Pa," came out. "Ah . . . Pa. Valora and I discovered our love for each other only yesterday."

"Well, it's about time," the elder man teased. "I thought you two would never come to that conclusion." He grinned.

"You don't mind?" Valora smiled demurely.

"Mind? I think it's wonderful. Now I'll really be able to call you my daughter." He gave her a big hug and shook his son's hand. "I'm very pleased, Tom."

Joel started to say something else, when he noticed horses and riders at a distance. "Could that be Paul and the sheriff . . . ?"

"And Suelena!" Valora turned quickly to see. "Oh, it is my sister with them. They are finally here!"

As the party drew closer, they hurried out to meet the returning two, plus one. Paul appeared an ashen color, but had a large grin spread across his face. "Hi everybody. The prodigal son hath returned, bringing along some very special friends, I might add."

Joel and Tom helped him off the horse. "Looks as if you've been in a battle. Come on in the house and tell us what happened."

"First, Pa, I want you to meet Suelena. She and the sheriff have been my lifesavers."

The sheriff helped the young woman down off her horse and Valora ran up to her sister. They squealed and hugged each other, while jumping up and down like excited little girls.

"So, you are Suelena. My! You're as pretty as your sister. I've heard so much about you that I feel I already know you," Joel greeted the tired young woman.

"Thank you, Sir." She felt a huge relief come over her. "We really need to get Paul inside. He's the one that saved my life. We've all had a terrible experience. We'll tell you about it in the house, all right?" Her face was full of concern.

Tom led the horses to the stable, while the rest of the party went inside the warm cozy home. Although wobbly on his feet, Paul dragged himself over to the couch and released his weary body on the comfortable sofa. Suelena situated herself by him on the floor. Sheriff Randal shared the story of the cougar attack, exaggerating just a tad, and also about the fine care Paul received at the farmhouse. It was then Paul found out about the note from Bonnie.

"We need to help Bonnie and the little ones as soon as we can," he said with deep emotion.

"You've got to get your strength back first, Paul. If you like, I'll ride over to Doc Rider's place and bring him back so he can check your wounds," the sheriff offered.

"No, really, Bob. I'll be fine now. Just a day or two of rest, and Valora's home cooking, I'll be as handsome as ever." A teasing grin appeared on his tired face.

"We do need to change his dressings and put some more of the poultice on his sores that Bonnie gave me," Suelena said with the same concern.

"Could you be hungry?" Valora looked at all three with a grin. "There's some chicken and dumplings left from dinner, and I baked a couple apple pies today."

"Mmm, sounds heavenly," Suelena exclaimed with the rest joining her in agreement. While Suelena changed Paul's stained cloths to fresh clean ones, Valora rewarmed the hungry trio's dinner.

Conversation around the table created a relaxed atmosphere. Valora recounted to the others the episode with the three men, the bears and the barn. The sheriff felt sorry he wasn't present when the dreadful occurrence took place. But, they all agreed he had helped save both Paul and Suelena from what would have been a horrible demise. Valora and Suelena then began catching up to date on their several months of separation. Joel and the men discussed the ranch. Consequently, the dialogue turned to Bonnie and the children.

The sheriff said he needed to do some searching of his records to ascertain if a wanted poster could be found on the man she called Buck. Then he wanted to summon some of the men in the area, deputize them into a posse to carry out what the law might require in releasing Bonnie and her offspring from the clutches of that scoundrel.

Tom and Paul both agreed the sheriff could count on them to be two of his deputies. Paul, of course, needed to get his strength back and be sure his wounds were healing well. He felt very sensitive to her needs because of the care she had given him, and insisted he should be a part in the rescue.

"We'd like you to spend the night with us, since it's getting late and you've had a rough trip," Joel suggested to Bob Randal.

"I really should be getting back to the office, but I will accept your kind hospitality this once. I am rather weary. We all are." He looked toward his companions and smiled. "And it probably is too late to do anything this evening."

"You can sleep in Mark's room upstairs. Suelena, for tonight you can share the room with Valora, if okay with you girls," the head of the house stated.

"Sounds perfect. We'll likely talk the night through!" Both girls giggled.

Being in this home where one obviously noticed the fondness and respect for one another instilled a feeling of warmth. Suelena realized her worrying about being accepted no longer remained a source of concern. She sensed her approval was very evident.

The following morning they found the two young women busy in the kitchen preparing the morning meal, when the men sat down at the table for breakfast.

"Smells mighty appetizing in here," the cheerful Bob Randal commented.

"I thought we'd have to drag you two out of bed this morning," Joel laughed.

"Funny, I just kept rambling on and on, and soon I didn't get any response from my sister. She must have been completely exhausted from the trip. So we did get a good night's rest," Valora said.

"Indeed, I was tired. The bed felt so inviting after sleeping out under the stars on the hard ground for several nights. I'm honestly sort of dreading the reverse trip already," Suelena interjected.

"How long will you be able to stay?" Joel asked.

"School was to begin this week. I should start back in a few days. The dear lady who is filling in for me stressed the need for my returning soon."

"Why don't you let me check about a teaching position in Cascadia? Then you wouldn't need to travel to Olympia at all. Our school here is much smaller, but the last I heard, we still lacked one educator," Joel suggested.

"Wel-l-l, I did tell Mrs. Wright I'd be back as soon as possible. Still, being close to Valora and friends sounds terrific." She thought for a minute, then said, "If it wouldn't put you out too much, Mr. McCalister, I'd certainly appreciate you asking if the position is still open. Then I could make my decision."

"I'll head into town immediately. I need to see if Doc Rider will come out and check on Paul's progress anyway." The older man seemed pleased.

"We can ride in together. I'd like to send off some wires and check over some files to see if there may be any information out on that Buck," the sheriff said.

First, Joel stopped by Doc Rider's office. The doctor stated he'd be pleased to see how Paul is recuperating, but it would be afternoon before he could leave town.

Indeed, a teaching position still remained unfilled for the younger grades in one classroom. Enticing qualified people to come to a small town such as Cascadia presented a problem. The head schoolmaster desired to talk with Suelena at her earliest convenience today, and if agreed, she would need to start teaching tomorrow morning, if possible.

Both Suelena and Valora found the favorable report Joel brought back a cause for rejoicing. After excusing herself, Suelena went to her room to make herself suitable for the interview. She styled her dark, shiny hair into a bun with steamers of curls trailing down the sides of her face. She then put on a crisp, white, long-sleeved blouse and a simple, but stylish, long, navy, blue skirt. "Do you think I will pass inspection?" she asked her new friends upon entering the living room.

Although feeling much improved Paul lay on the couch and expressed his opinion. "You are as lovely as ever. I'd like to ride with you into town, but I'd better stay here in case the doctor comes."

Tom and Valora glanced at each other and winked. Little cupid angels started flying through Valora's imagination. *Wouldn't that be a nice combination. . . . Paul and Suelena?* she thought. "I'll ride in with Suelena. I can pick up a few supplies, while she's being interviewed," she said.

Suddenly she remembered something. "Oh, wait one minute!" She ran into the bedroom, coming back with a small gift, wrapped package. "I want you to have this."

"A gift!" Suelena quickly opened it. "It's beautiful. Mama had a broach much like this. Oh, Valora, you're so thoughtful. I'll cherish this forever . . . but, I didn't bring you anything." She held back a tear.

Valora smiled. "You're here. That's all that matters. Please, let me help put it on."

The beauty of the emerald necklace transformed her plain but neat outfit into an affect of elegance. The sisters hugged each other, then Tom entered the room. "The team is hitched to the wagon. My, don't you look pretty, Suelena."

"Why, thank you," she smiled shyly. "You're all so kind.

111

We'd better get going. Please say a little prayer that I make the right impression and decision."

An older, authoritarian-looking gentleman sat at a desk. There wasn't much hair on his balding head. Dark-rimmed spectacles hung low on his nose. A frown crossed his forehead. The thick, neatly, trimmed mustache barely concealed a stern mouth. Suelena felt somewhat overwhelmed and a little frightened by his appearance, and decided the students surely didn't get away with any mischief when he entered a room.

He soon put the young lady at ease, when he spoke, "Come in, Miss Dillon. I'm Charles Carlton, the head school-master. Won't you please sit down?" He introduced himself, his speech and mannerisms showed kindness.

The interview went very well. He found her genuinely qualified for the position. If she accepted, she would be teaching first through sixth grade students, which she favored . . . in one classroom. Mr. Carlton would teach the older grades. He did have them all in one classroom until he could find another teacher. The pay was smaller, but she didn't really care for now. Her only regret was having to break the news to Mrs. Wright in Olympia; a telegraph wire would be the quickest way. Then she could follow up with a letter explaining her desire to be close to her sister, and the opportunity of teaching right here in Cascadia. She felt confident the larger town would have a relatively easier time replacing a teacher than Cascadia had in obtaining one.

After a few moments of deep thought and silent prayer, she expressed her appreciation for the consultation, and accepted the placement offered to her. They both smiled, shook hands and he told her he looked forward to working with her. "Beginning tomorrow morning," he stressed once again.

It amazed Valora to find how quickly news had spread in the small settlement. Mrs. Jones already had been informed about the occurrence with the three dangerous men and Suelena's arrival. However, she found pleasure in acknowledging that the town showed relief since the malicious ogres would never more be a threat to the two young women, or the townsfolk as well. She also found Mrs. Jones a very likeable person, who showed evidence that she did not appreciate gossip. On the other hand, she wanted Valora to recognize that the town did care, and supported her and her sister, and offered their availability to assist them in any way they could provide. Valora hoped that when the sheriff made the decision to gather a posse, they would recall the offer.

As she started to gather her supplies, Sheriff Randal happened to enter the general store, "May I lend some aid to my charming friend?" he offered.

"That would please me very much, thank you," she said. "Some of these items are much too heavy for us wee little women. I'm glad you happened along." She found he enjoyed teasing; and he did, as a wide grin spread across his face.

"Have you acquired any information on Buck yet?" She asked, as he loaded her purchases on the buckboard.

"It will take at least a couple days before I receive a reply from the telegrams. I may have a poster on him though. Composite drawings aren't always reliable. But, from the way the bulletin reads, he just may be the man we're looking for. I sure don't want to wait too long before going back to the farmhouse. It's no telling what he might do to Bonnie and her offspring, now that he knows a sheriff has been out there." His pleasant facial expression turned into one of concern.

"Here comes Suelena. She has a cheerful smile on her face. I hope that means good news," her sister remarked.

"Hi, there. Any beneficial tidings yet?" Suelena acknowledged the sheriff.

"I was just telling Valora, there's a possibility we may

have some information on the man, Buck. I'm waiting on reports back from the wires I've sent off to confirm it."

"How did the interview go?" Valora anxiously asked.

"Very well. I am now your employed sister once again. I'll be teaching the first six grades . . . starting tomorrow!" She rolled her eyes and grinned.

"Terrific!" Valora and Bob exclaimed at the same instant.

"I really need to find a room at the boarding house, so I can be closer to school," Suelena said.

"I'm sorry, ma'am. We have no such place in Town. I make my residence in a room adjoining the Sheriff's Office that I built," Bob reported. "There is a hotel. However, it's right above the saloon. No place for a lady such as yourself. I did stay there while building the jail and my room. But I wouldn't advise it for you."

"Oh, dear. Now what should I do? I can't impose on the McCalisters any more."

"They'll delight in having you," Valora assured her. "We could eventually find a place where we could live together."

At the dinner table that evening, Valora and Suelena shared their news of the day, and the necessity of finding a place for Suelena to live.

"Of course, there's no problem. We want you to live here with us, as long as you'd enjoy staying . . . but . . . only under one condition . . ." All eyes were on the older man. "That you quit calling me Mr. McCalister." Joel grinned broadly.

"Okay, Papa Mack." Suelena presented him a grateful smile in return.

The name pleased him immensely. "You can take Mark's room, so you will have a place to call your own and study in peace. He can double up with one of his brothers when he comes home, since he won't be here much while in college."

"Your kindness towards Valora and I is overwhelming. I sincerely hope we can repay you some day."

"You will. I'm certain. You will!"

Ten

The girls arose with the sun the following morning. Valora dressed quickly and hurried on over to the Judsons' to feed the chickens before fixing breakfast. Several days had gone by since last seeing the ones she felt so much affection for. Sarah started walking out the door to do her chores, when she noticed Valora ride in. Sarah ran over to the chicken pen, wanting to hear the latest news from her friend. Valora greeted her warmly and shared all the recent events, while fulfilling her task of taking care of the feathery fowls.

"I'm excited about meeting your sister. I know it will be nice for you to have another woman in the house." Sarah appeared a little downhearted today.

"Is something bothering you, Sarah?"

"I suppose." Sarah toyed with a rock, kicking it with her foot, her head cast down. "Sometimes there's so much to do. I guess I just miss Mama. I'm so glad you came by, Valora. I know I shouldn't complain."

"Have you heard from Mark lately?"

"It's been a couple weeks now. He's so busy with his schooling and he's barely getting started for the year. He said he would be home for Thanksgiving, but that seems so far off."

Valora thought a minute and then came up with a suggestion she hoped would help to lift her spirits. "Why don't you bring Susie and Kaye by for lunch? The twins and older children will be in school. The men said they wouldn't be here for lunch. They have work needing to be done away from the house and would just take a lunch with them today. The girls haven't seen Gruffy in a long time. He misses his companion. Do they know about Big Nose being killed?"

"Yes, I had to tell them. They cried so hard. Thank you for the invitation. I really would enjoy coming. I know the girls will be thrilled. Okay. We'll be there . . . and I'll bring one of my special cakes."

"No. I don't want you to bring a thing except the girls. You deserve a day off. I'd better be heading back. I want to see Suelena before she leaves for her new teaching position." Valora mounted her horse and waved good-bye as she started home, trusting everything would be all right with her friend.

"Come as soon as you can after the other children get off to school," she hollered back at her friend, waving bye.

Suelena took her time dressing for her first day of school, while hoping and wondering if the students would accept her. A freshly starched powder, blue blouse blended nicely with the navy skirt she had worn yesterday for the job interview. The colors brought out the deep, sky blue in her eyes, which shone with excitement. She had styled her hair in the favorite fashionable bun. By the time she finished and went into the kitchen, she found Valora already preparing breakfast for the family.

"Are you nervous?" her sister asked.

"First day on a new job, and not knowing the children, yes, I must admit, I am feeling a mite bit weak in the knees."

"They'll love you. And you'll do just fine," Valora encouraged her cheerfully.

"You're probably inclined to be a little biased, nevertheless, that's okay. I need all the encouragement I can get." Suelena smiled, feeling a bit more confident. "I could have used another day or two to rest up and visit with you, but when opportunities come our way, it's best to take advantage of them when you can."

Suelena left shortly after helping her sister clean up the kitchen. She preferred to allow plenty of time to ride into town in order to locate the livery stables. Pleased to find the stables close to the schoolhouse, she left her horse, Blaze.

Not long after setting up the room to her satisfaction, the school bell began to ring. As she pealed out the classroom door into the hallway, she spied a little girl hanging on to a rope with all of her strength. Her face revealed a proud grin, giving away the satisfaction she was experiencing, while riding the rope up and down, as the bell peeled out the loud clanging sounds. Suelena smiled and after a spell offered to help the girl off the rope, convincing her of the need to be in the room for class to begin.

As the men were about ready to leave the house to tackle their tasks on the ranch for the day, they grabbed the lunches Valora had packed for them; then Tom asked Paul if he could speak with him a moment. "We can talk on our way to the barn," he suggested.

"Sure. Whatcha got on your mind, big brother?"

"I'm uncertain how to begin." He let out a sigh. "I need to discuss something very important with you. Ahh, Paul, I know you have had some fond feelings for Valora, and I need to know exactly how you feel about her." He looked at his younger brother with a serious expression on his face.

"Well, yes. I really do care for Valora. For a while I thought I might even be in love with her. Yet . . . umm, on the return trip from Olympia with Suelena . . . well, I sort of have mixed emotions now. They are both extremely beautiful ladies, and I'm not sure exactly how I feel. Why do you ask?" His features expressed curiosity.

"I realized you cared about Valora not long after she came to live in our home, so I backed off. But, Paul, while you were away something happened between Valora and me. We didn't plan it, believe me. Paul . . . what I'm finding difficult to say is . . . well . . . I wouldn't want to hurt our kinship in anyway . . . but, Valora and I discovered our feelings for each other are not just a brother-sister kind of relationship, or even merely good friends. Paul . . . we love each other." He searched his brother's face for approval.

Paul stood silent, as if he couldn't comprehend the words he heard his older brother speaking. A change of emotion displaying dejection began to fill his eyes; then he slowly walked away as if laden with a heavy burden. Tom didn't know whether to go after his brother or leave him alone. Finally, he decided it best to let him be, to search through his feelings.

Valora spent the morning straightening up the house and preparing a special lunch for her guests. At times she, too, had recurrences when she would feel overcome with an intense loss of her folks; she could understand her friend's grievous feelings. It's strange how you can be susceptible to loneliness, even when there's people you care for around. Then at other times you can experience enjoyment in being alone, to think over your thoughts and take time to dream.

The morning breezed by so swiftly. When she heard the clatter of little feet on the porch, then knocking on the door, she was ready, yet she pretended to be surprised." Well, I declare. Who do we have here?"

"It's me, Susie . . . and Kaye . . . and Sarah. You know who we are, Miss Valora," Susie giggled.

"My goodness. What a nice surprise. Do come in, ladies. I just happen to have some lunch prepared, and thought I would have to eat it all by myself. Would you perhaps be hungry?" she teased.

"Yesss!" The girls peeled out, as they gave her a big hug. Sarah's countenance appeared much more cheerful than it had shown earlier. Sometimes, understanding and encouragement from a friend can be the best medicine one receives.

Following lunch and kitchen clean up, the girls became anxious to visit their friend, Gruffy. His actions were those of delight, when he saw them coming as he pranced back and forth in the pen. Tom had made a collar for his neck, so Valora attached a rope to the collar and suggested they take him for a walk, well, more of a pull than a walk. The bear seemed to sense their love and his need to be gentle with his playmates.

The two girls, the women, and the bear took a path that led up a hillside overlooking the ranch. Valora and Sarah found a perfect site to relax under a huge elm tree, glorying in the mass of colorful leaves. After removing the rope from Gruffy's collar, it allowed the children and their pet to romp as freely as they wished in the fresh, smelling grass and fallen autumn leaves. Golden sunbeams brightened up the clear, sunny sky. The young women lay back on a blanket, which they had spread upon the ground and watched the puffy, white clouds drift slowly by. An eagle soared across the sky, while their imaginations formed different shapes out of the clouds.

After a time Valora broke the silence, "I've been giving some deep thought about our little bear friend. He's getting so big and more restless since Big Nose died. With fall in the air it won't be long till he'll be experiencing the need to hibernate for the winter. His injured foot has mended nicely. I'm thinking, for his sake, it would be wise to let our dear captive go free. Do you think the girls would understand, Sarah?"

"Let's call them over and talk with them," she suggested.

The girls, still full of exuberance, came running when called with Gruffy close behind. "Susie and Kaye, I have something very important to discuss with you," Valora started the conversation. "You see how much Gruffy enjoys being free?

Sometimes he gets so restless, always penned up and he misses his brother . . . so . . . what do you think we should do?"

"Welll . . . maybe you should let him sleep in your bed. Then he wouldn't be so lonely anymore," Kaye, the four year old offered. "I sleep with my Teddy bear."

"No, silly. He's too big. Miss Valora wouldn't have any room. How about a bigger pen?" Susie pronounced.

"What if we took him back where we found him and let him go where ever he wanted?" Sarah hinted.

"Nooo!" Both girls cried out. "We'd never get to see him again!"

"Let's stop and think about this," Valora interjected. "Gruffy soon will be getting even bigger and some day he might want to have a family of his own. How would he ever meet another bear, if we kept him penned up all the time? I love Gruffy, too. But he really needs to live the kind of life bears enjoy . . . being free and roaming the woods in his kind of natural surroundings. Bears like to play in streams and lakes and climb trees. It's their nature to be constantly moving around, hunting through rotted logs, crevices and boulders for honey and foods they enjoy eating. You wouldn't want to be cooped up all day with nothing to do but wait for someone to come along to play with, would you? If we keep him from doing the things God created him to do, we wouldn't be very good friends . . . do you think?" Valora tried her best to explain in a way they might understand.

"I guess not. But do we have to let him go today?" Susie wasn't quite convinced they should give up their playmate yet.

"Since it's getting late now, we could wait one more week. Let's plan a picnic, like the day we found him. We could arrange it for Saturday, so the twins can come, too. And maybe Suelena, my sister, would like to join us. I want you all to meet her."

With some hesitation the girls finally agreed. "Okay.

Next Saturday we have a date. You'll have to be strong, and remember, sometimes it's better to let the ones we love go . . . for their sake," Valora said, as she looked at Sarah, then adding very gently, "And, sometimes we have to give up the ones we love, for our sake."

Sarah knew exactly what she meant. She tried to be strong for her father, when her mother died, all the while keeping her own feelings hidden in her heart. Now the time had come to release those feelings and go on with her own life. Yes, she thought, there was added responsibilities for her, but God promised He would not give us more than we can bear . . . physically, spiritually or mentally. And with God's help we can learn through all kinds of experiences that touch our lives. We never quit loving someone because they have died. The memories will always be there to treasure in our hearts. However, we must not dwell on them. Life does have its heartaches at times. Unfortunately, death is a part of life . . . the sad part. Still, when the sun rises and brings forth a new day, we need to look for the challenges that come our way. Opportunities can blossom us into maturity and build character. Sarah felt grateful to have a friend like Valora, who cared enough to uphold and encourage her to grow, and decided how thankful we should be for the friends God gives to us.

At the supper table that evening, Valora shared her decision to set Gruffy free. They all felt it to be a wise choice. In truth, Papa Mack had often times concerned himself about the proper way to suggest such an idea, and found a feeling of relief when Valora broke the news.

Joel also noticed a tension during the meal this evening between Tom and Paul and wondered what the problem might be. All three of his sons had always gotten along remarkably well, for which he deemed fortunate. Of course, as youngsters they had their bickering. As they matured into men though, they cultivated a mutual respect for each other.

Not wanting to intrude on his grown sons' disagreements, he decided not to interfere by asking too many questions. Instead, he would let them work out the situation on their own, unless they decided to ask his advice.

In lieu of his decision, he turned and asked, "How was your first day of school, Suelena?" Joel felt truly interested.

"The boys and girls behaved very well, except one little guy. He's as cute as a cuddly kitten, but he sure tried my patience. When I began to speak, he forever interrupted. If I turned my back, he would throw spit balls. At recess he caused one fight after another. I'm sorry to say, he spent most of the afternoon standing in a corner."

"What's his name?" Paul asked.

"David Judson."

"Oh, dear, that's one of the twins . . . Sarah's brother. He never had been a problem before. After his mother, Emma Judson, became ill his grades started to go downhill. He had to be kept back a year in his studies, while his twin brother was advanced to the third level. He probably isn't getting enough attention at home, and maybe he's feeling a little ashamed of having to take second grade over," Joel replied.

"Thank you for telling me all this," Suelena spoke. "I believe I can handle the situation better now that I know the circumstances. I'll find something he enjoys doing and see if I can help him through this critical time in his life. Children can be affected by so many things. Some adjust to change in life better than others. Evidently the other twin is doing all right. It's up to us as adults to recognize the problems and try to help where we can."

"Sarah and I are planning a picnic in about a week . . . next Saturday, actually. How about you coming along, Suelena? We want the twins to come, as well as Susie and Kaye."

"Sounds like fun. Maybe we can find something special

for David to do," Suelena remarked with excitement in her voice.

"I hear someone riding up," Tom said at the same time, walking over to the window. "It's Sheriff Randal. Maybe he has some news."

Tom escorted the sheriff into the house and offered him a chair at the table with the rest of the family. Seeing the empty, but obviously used plates, he said, "Aw shucks. I just missed supper."

"We still have some wild blackberry pie, if you'd care for some," Valora offered.

"Now I sure can't turn that down, although I'm really here on business. I'm getting together a posse to bring Buck in. We'll be heading out at sun-up in the morning. Tom and Paul had said they would join me. Do you feel up to it, Paul?"

"I'm feeling back to my old self again. Sure, I'll ride with you," he agreed with no hesitation.

Tom also said to include him as a member of the posse, and asked, "What did you find out about that scoundrel, my friend?"

"He's wanted in several states for robbery, holding up a bank and killing a sheriff in Wyoming. Who knows what all he's been charged with? I'm afraid it may be a dangerous mission. I want you men to be aware of the risk ahead." He wrinkled his forehead in an anxious but inquiring expression.

The girls and Joel became concerned for Paul; but he insisted on going along with the sheriff, Tom and the rest. He made plain his desire to take part in helping Bonnie and her children in any way he could.

Tom asked, "How many more men do you need? Some of our ranch hands may be willing to join us."

"I have one other man from town, Slim Dobbs, and you two. Probably two more will be enough."

124

"Let's check right now and see who will go." Tom arose from his chair.

The sheriff gulped down his last bite of pie, thanked them for their hospitality, then he and Tom went to the barracks and found two husky men willing to volunteer. "We'll meet at my office at six in the morning," Bob Randal told the men.

As the sheriff rode off into the night towards town, Paul joined Tom outside. "I've been giving what we talked about this morning a great deal of thought. At first, I guess my pride over shadowed me. I felt both hurt and angry with you for taking away my chance with Valora. Then I got to thinking on what I'd said this morning. I thought I was in love, and realized what I felt must have been infatuation.

"Tom, if you love Valora . . . if you both share that same love for each other, who am I to stand in your way? I want you both to be happy. And for what it's worth, you have my blessings. Besides, I've got some fond feelings for Suelena. She's kinda rubbed off on me. Maybe there could be something growing between us." His eyes began to sparkle as he broke into a smile.

"Thanks, Paul. We've always had a good relationship. I wouldn't want anything to come between us, not even Valora."

They gave each other a brotherly hug, then shook hands and walked back inside the house. Joel was pouring himself a cup of coffee and noticed the strained relations between his sons had disappeared. "You men be careful tomorrow. I don't want anything to happen to my sons." His voice filled with emotion.

"We'll be fine. I'll look after Paul, and he'll look after me." He grabbed his brother's shoulder, giving it a squeeze.

"That's what brothers are for." Paul grinned and teasingly slugged his brother in the arm.

Eleven

Everyone rose before dawn's first light the next morning. Valora and Suelena busied themselves in the kitchen fixing a wholesome breakfast. They had already prepared a lunch for all the men making the journey to attempt the rescue of Bonnie and her youngsters, before the men sat down at the table to eat.

"I have something I would like for you to give the children." Suelena handed Paul two small packages. "Please don't take any unnecessary chances. We want you all to come back safe and well." She smiled. "We'll be praying for you."

"Don't worry. We'll be fine." Paul gave her a kiss on the cheek. Suelena blushed.

Tom kissed Valora good-bye in front of the family, embarrassing her, then shook his father's hand. Joel gave each of his sons a big, bear hug. "Yes, we'll certainly be praying for God to ride alongside each one of you," he said with assurance.

Sheriff Randal and Dobbs sat mounted on their horses waiting in front of the office. They greeted the brothers and their ranch hands, when the four rode up. The sheriff swore in his men, as they solemnly declared to uphold the law, and gave each a deputy's badge. He informed them of the plan he had created, then declared, "Let's head out!"

No one else could be seen on the street, while they rode out of town, picking up the pace at the edge of the settlement. Each man felt the urgency of the situation for which they had agreed to invest their lives, if necessary, to help in the rescue.

Time went by quickly, as they rode fast and hard. Soon the sheriff brought the posse to a halt. "The farm seems closer to Cascadia then I remembered. 'Course Paul was in bad shape and we had to take it easy getting him home. The farmhouse is just a short distance over that ridge. Paul and I will go on up to the door like we planned. Hopefully Buck won't suspect anything out of the ordinary, if he only sees us. As soon as we can get inside, you circle the house, then you know what to do."

Paul and the sheriff rode their horses closer to the farmhouse. As they anticipated, Buck came out the door with his shotgun. "What-da-ya-want? Oh, it's you guys again."

"We happened to be in the area and wanted to stop by and thank you once more for the kind hospitality you showed us a few days back," the sheriff answered, trying hard to appear as pleasant as he could muster.

"Okay. You said it. Now get out'a here." Buck evidently found enjoyment in being hateful.

"Wait! I brought the children gifts from Suelena," Paul quickly interrupted, thankful for Suelena's gesture.

"They're not feeling good," Buck growled.

"Please, I won't take but a minute, then we'll be on our way," Paul pleaded with a little impatience in his voice. At that moment little Charlie came to the door with a bloody nose. Without a doubt, he had been crying.

"Get back in there, kid." The burly man pushed him.

Bonnie quickly made her way to the door with Evie hanging on to her skirt. "Let them in please, Buck." Her eyes and the little girl's were filled with despair. Bonnie's face revealed several additional bruises and scars.

The sheriff pushed the door open. "Surely you won't mind us bringing the children gifts," he said.

"I have the presents in my saddle bag. Come on, Charlie and Evie. Let's go get the gifts." Paul grabbed the children before Buck could say anything. The big man tried to stop them, but the sheriff took a hold of his arm and held him at bay.

While hastening the youngsters toward his horse, Paul whispered, "After I hand you the presents, I want you to run as fast as you can into the woods." Paul pointed in the direction, where the other men had hid themselves and the horses behind the brush and trees, while waiting further instructions. "My brother, Tom, and some other nice men will be there to help you."

He reached in the saddlebag and handed the gifts to each child, then spoke in a low voice, "Now run!" He watched until they were at a safe distance, then hurried back to the house.

Upon entering, the sheriff said, "I have come to arrest you for robbery, kidnaping and murdering a sheriff in Wyoming, as well as Bonnie's husband."

All of a sudden Buck grabbed Bonnie and held a knife to her throat. "You come one step closer and I'll kill her." The expression on his face left no doubt he meant business.

Both men froze in alarm. Without hesitation, Bonnie kicked the big man; she bit her captor on the arm, startling the brute. The sheriff grasped Buck's arm holding the knife and pulled it away from her throat. Paul shot his gun into the ceiling, not wanting to chance hitting the wrong person. The three other deputies heard the shot and immediately ran toward the house. Dobbs had been instructed to stay behind with the children. The sheriff and the outlaw struggled. Finally, Randal jerked the criminal's arms behind his back and quickly fastened handcuffs around Buck's wrists.

Tom hollered to Dobbs to bring the children to the house, as Bonnie ran to collect them. With outstretched arms, she drew them to herself, hugging and kissing each one. The little family, along with Dobbs, entered the house.

"I knew you would come." She looked at the sheriff, then Paul. "I'm so thankful you didn't forget us." She stared back at

Buck. "He's a horrible man. He beat us. Much of the time he would get to drinking and break up what furniture we had, and, and . . ." she broke down and wept.

Sheriff Randal, filled with compassion for this woman, took her in his arms and spoke soothingly, "It's all right now, Bonnie. He won't touch you or the youngsters any more. We'll see to that. We want you to come back to Cascadia with us. I talked with the doctor in town. He wants to meet you, and said possibly hire you as his assistant."

"Oh, I don't know what to say." Her bewildered expression couldn't take in all that had happened so quickly. "Is it really over?" She shook her head in disbelief.

"Just come with us. You don't have to make any other decisions right now," the sheriff attempted to assure her.

"Okay if I get a few things together? We don't have much, but we'll need some clean clothes." The sheriff nodded a yes, as Bonnie went on into the bedroom for their clothes, knowing without hesitation what the answer would be.

"Mommy, Mommy. Look what Miss Suelena sent me." Evie followed her mother into the room, while she held up the cute little doll with blond curly hair.

"She sent me this." Charlie stood at the doorway, holding up something in his hand. His expression showed he wasn't quite sure if he liked his gift or not.

"That's a harmonica. I'll teach you how to play it." Tom went to him and grinned, glad for the change in the atmosphere.

"Oh. A a-monica? That's neat." Charlie's quizzical look turned into a big smile, showing two missing front teeth.

Tom played him a tune on the mouthpiece, while Bonnie gathered up their things. Charlie's face really lit up after hearing the harmonica make such a beautiful sound. "Can I try?" Tom handed the musical instrument to him and he blew and blew, thrilled with the noise that come out of his new treasure.

129

Bonnie came back from the bedroom with a small frame, holding a photograph, "I'd like to show you a picture of my husband. We had so many plans for this place when we moved here. Now I don't care if I ever see this house again. So many terrible things have happened since we came." She shook her head, tears welling up in her eyes again.

"Do you have any horses in the barn or saddles?" The sheriff asked, after glancing at the photo.

"We only have one horse and one saddle," the woman replied.

"Well, I'd make Buck walk, if it wasn't for slowing the rest of us down. We'll have to let him ride it. You ride with me, Bonnie."

"Charlie can ride with me," Tom offered.

"Then I'll take Evie with me," Paul added, smiling down at the little girl and taking her hand. She looked up at him with a trusting grin on her cherub face.

"We'd better get on our way." The sheriff pushed Buck out the door. "Bill, would you saddle up the horse in the barn?"

"Sure. Glad to." Bill was one of the McCalister's ranch hands. He moved in the direction of the rundown building, soon coming back with an undernourished black horse.

"His name is Blackie," Charlie told them.

"Well, Blackie, I hope you can make the trip to a new life. I promise we'll fatten you up." The sheriff gave him a rub on his nose. Everyone chuckled except Buck, who was being forced onto the horse's back. The horse tried to shy away from him, as if afraid of the man.

The party finally set out for Cascadia along the winding trail through the woods, over hills, crossing a river on a wooden bridge. Each one became lost in their own thoughts and at peace the whole ordeal soon would be over without too

130

much of a hassle. Well, everyone except Charlie. He played his new 'monica.'

About halfway through the journey, Sheriff Randal mentioned, "Let's take time out to eat our lunch the girls fixed for us." No argument could be heard. There were plenty of ham sandwiches, carrot sticks, boiled eggs, and cookies for everyone.

When they finally arrived in town, Sheriff Randal locked up the prisoner in one of the cells. Dobbs offered to stay at the jail, since he lived in town, wasn't married and didn't have a family waiting for him. Tom, Paul and their two hands directed their mounts toward the McCalister ranch. "We'll be seeing you soon," Paul called back to Bonnie and the children.

"Thank you so much for everything," she answered, an expression of gladness and relief shown on her face. This was the first time she had genuinely smiled in months. The children waved their good-byes.

"I'd like to take you by Doc Rider's office," Bob Randal suggested to the mother and her family.

They walked across the dirt street to the doctor's office and found he had already left for home. "It's just a short distance to his house. I'll rent a carriage down at the stable. Stay put and I'll be right back." Bonnie tried to refrain him, saying they could walk. But he mounted his horse leading Blackie by the reins. Bonnie and the children huddled together outside the jail, not wanting to go inside with Buck in there.

Soon the sheriff rode up in the carriage, loaded the family and went out to the doctor's large home. Beautiful baskets of flowers hung along the eaves of the long porch. The doctor answered their knock at the door, expressed pleasure in meeting them and invited his guests into the lovely home. Mrs. Rider brought some cookies and coffee for the adults and milk for the children, while their guests sat around the dining table.

"I understand you're a nurse?" the doctor began the conversation.

"Yes. I started out studying to become a doctor. But, then I met and fell in love with my husband before I completed my studies," Bonnie answered. "Joshua wanted to come out west soon after we married. He always loved farming. We traveled to Kansas and farmed a while. Both Charlie and Evalene were born there. Still he had an earnest desire to come all the way west. One day a friend showed him an article in a newspaper about a farm for sale in the Washington Territory at an attractive price. We bought the little farm, sight unseen. He didn't even show disappointment when we found the house in such shambles. All he could see was the potential. We really worked hard trying to get a crop started. Most of our money was spent on the purchase of the farm. We planned to fix up the house with the proceeds from our harvest. Then Buck showed up. Buck and my husband got into a terrible fight. That's when he killed my Joshua." Bonnie started to weep. The children began to cry, stirring the sympathy of Bob Randal and the Riders with compassion for this family. Mrs. Rider put her arms around the younger woman and attempted to comfort Bonnie until she could compose her emotions.

After a while Mrs. Rider asked to see her husband alone in the kitchen. They excused themselves, then Mrs. Rider said, "Honey, we never had any children of our own. Let's make a home for Bonnie and her family here with us. We have plenty of bedrooms upstairs. Hardly ever are those rooms used." Her eyes were pleading with her husband.

The doctor rubbed his chin for a minute, pondering over the idea. He liked the thought. "It would be nice to have her close by to help with my practice. But would you mind looking after the young'uns?" He gave her a questioning glance.

"Mind!? Why I'd be in heaven!"

"You're sure now, dear? This would be a big step to take.

132

Our lives won't be the same with little children running around." The doctor wanted her to think clearly about all sides of the situation.

"We'll take it one day at a time. But I'm sure we can all be happy as a family," the missus replied with a touching smile on her lips.

They went back into the dining area. The sheriff held Charlie propped on his lap giggling. Evie sat on Bonnie's lap, playing with her new doll.

"The doctor and I discussed something very important. If you don't agree, we'll understand. Bonnie, my dear, we would like you and your children to live here with us. We have plenty of room. You can make the entire upstairs your home."

Bonnie's mouth flew open. "Live here with you?"

"Now, you don't have to stay forever, and don't feel like you have to say yes. We'd love to have you, but . . ."

"Dear Doctor and Mrs. Rider, you are so very kind," Bonnie interrupted. "You've all been so good to me and my family already." She looked at Bob Randal.

"Well, I'd say it's about time you had something good happen to you for a change," the sheriff exclaimed with a big grin.

"What do you say?" the doctor asked.

"Can we stay Mommy? Can we?" the children begged.

"If it's not putting you out too much," Bonnie replied. "But I won't have any money for rent until I sell my place, and that could take some time."

"You can work it off by being my nurse. I've been in need of an assistant for a long time," the doctor encouraged her.

"This is just too good to be true. I'd love to get back into the medical field. And I'd be honored to be your nurse, Doctor Rider." The tears began to fill her eyes once more, but this time . . . tears of joy.

"Then that settles it. Why don't you bring in the family's

133

belongings, Sheriff?" The sheriff immediately rose from his chair to get her little roll of clothing and brought it in.

"Is that all?" Mrs. Rider asked.

"I'm afraid so, ma'am," the sheriff said.

"Well, we'll do something about that tomorrow," Mrs Rider asserted.

"I guess I'd better get going. I need to relieve Dobbs at the jail. I'll be seeing ya'll," the sheriff said, as he started walking toward the door.

"Wait!" Bonnie ran over and kissed his cheek and gave him a big hug. "I don't know how to thank you for all you've done for us."

"You just did, ma'am," and gave her a wink.

Twelve

Rain! Rain! Rain! Some weeks that's all it seems to want to do. Valora felt obligated to plan the upcoming picnic, but the weather made it impossible to envision eating out of doors, when all she could think of was a drippy sky. The rain really didn't pour down, just constantly drizzled. Suelena found the weather even more miserable, as she rode her horse to and from school.

One evening nearing the end of the week after the women had retired to their rooms, the three McCalisters sat relaxing around a cozy fire discussing the issues of the day. During the conversation, Tom mentioned he had overheard one of his men express that a nearby neighbor has a carriage for sale.

"Hmm, do you know anything about it? What kind of shape is it? Does it have a good cover on top?" Joel showed interest.

"I don't know any of those answers, but there may be value in checking out its worth," Tom responded. "A carriage sure would be a convenience for the girls, especially with the cool nights of fall beginning to settle in. Suelena could use the vehicle for traveling to and from school and Valora for shopping."

"Why don't I take Suelena into Cascadia tomorrow in the buckboard, then I can inquire about the buggy?" Paul suggested.

"That would be a superb idea. Let's not mention anything

to the girls until we see if it's worthwhile. Maybe we can surprise them," remarked the older brother.

Suelena wasn't overly exuberant about getting out of her warm comfortable bed the following morning. She could see there had been no letup in the rainy weather, when she peered out of her bedroom window. Normally, she enjoyed the view overlooking tall evergreens mingled in with dogwood and madrona trees. Even the little wren perched on a limb by the windowsill warbling its morning call didn't perk up her enthusiasm.

Eventually she joined her sister in the kitchen. The aroma of coffee already brewing on the wood-burning stove livened up her taste buds. She poured herself a cup of the savoring brew, then shared in the duties of preparing the morning meal.

Paul joined the women in the kitchen. "I'll be glad to take you to work in the buckboard this morning, if you like, Suelena. Then you can at least hold an umbrella over your head to help keep dry."

"You don't need to do that. I'll be fine." She smiled, pleased with the offer.

"I have some business in town which will probably take a good part of the day, so it won't be any problem at all." He encouraged a "yes" response.

Joel overheard the conversation, as he entered the room. "You'd better take him up on the offer. He believes it's drudgery traveling to town too often." He tried to tempt her even more.

"I admit the change would be nice, and I certainly would enjoy the company," she said. "Maybe we could go a little early. I would like to stop by the Riders' and say hi to Bonnie a few minutes before school. I haven't seen Charlie in class yet, and I'm sure he should be in first grade."

136

Paul agreed, as the family sat down for the meal. "We'd better get going right away."

"You go ahead and leave, Suelena. I'll take care of the kitchen," Valora suggested.

"Thank you, dear sister. I'll clean the kitchen this evening." Suelena offered her assistance with a smile.

Soon Paul was helping Suelena into the wagon. By now the drizzle had turned into a steady downpour. She made an attempt to hold an umbrella over both of them, causing her to have to sit closer to her handsome escort. The wind tried to blow the umbrella away several times, nearly turning it inside out. Water from the parasol dipped down Paul's neck, leaving him wetter than if she hadn't held it over him, but he didn't complain. They laughed and teased each other, which made the trip into town go by all too swiftly.

After arriving at the Riders' home, she squeezed Paul's arm and gave him a peck on the cheek. As she started to climb down from the buckboard, her skirt caught on to the wheel. Down she went smack dab into a mud puddle. She started to get up, but slipped and fell down again. In alarm she scrunched her face into a frown. Her clothes were covered in mud. Paul jumped off the wagon and ran to her rescue. While helping to pick her up, he slipped and almost fell too.

At first she felt terribly embarrassed and looked so pitiful. Paul tried hard to hold back a grin. Pretty soon they both broke out in laughter. "I do believe I'm more soaked than if I would have ridden Blaze into town," she finally stammered.

Bonnie had come to the door, upon hearing the commotion outside. After opening it, she found her two dripping wet friends grinning at her. "What in the world happened to you two?" she exclaimed.

"Well, I fell in a mud puddle." Suelena had a comical expression on her muddy face.

"Come in. You look a sight! We'd better get those wet clothes off you before you catch your death of cold."

"Thank you," Suelena began to explain. "Paul brought me by to see Charlie. I hope I can take him to school with me." It was more of a question.

"Bonnie, you look like a different woman." Paul stared at her. His mouth had fallen open in amazement.

She had styled her light, brown hair with bangs, having brushed back the sides, catching the hair with a pink ribbon at the back of her head. Curls flowed down her shoulders and proceeded on down the middle of her back. She wore a plain white high-collared blouse tucked into a long black, full skirt. Color began to brighten up her unscarred complexion. Bonnie appeared downright attractive. What a change from the last time they had seen her with such a bruised and beaten up face, ragged clothes and unkempt hair.

She nodded her head shyly and smiled at Paul, then he noticed Doc Rider in the kitchen and walked towards the room to talk with him. In the meantime Bonnie aimed Suelena upstairs to her domain.

"Mrs. Rider bought some material. We've been sewing clothes for the children and me. I didn't want to send Charlie to school until he had a decent outfit. Now he has several, and since you're here, it would be nice to get him started in school."

After washing up, Bonnie encouraged her friend to borrow an outfit she had recently sewn. Suelena didn't have a choice, since her own clothes looked such a mess. Bonnie was a little smaller, but Suelena managed to fit into the dark skirt and white blouse fashioned similar to the outfit Bonnie was wearing. After redressing her hairdo, she declared her readiness to leave for school.

They found Charlie downstairs playing a tune on his "monica" for Paul. Doc Rider had taught him a simple melody.

Evie stood on a chair helping Mema, Mrs. Rider's new name, with the dishes.

"Charlie, how would you like to go to school with Miss Suelena this morning?" Bonnie asked her son. He did look adorable in the new blue pants and matching shirt she had finished sewing just yesterday.

"Yesss!" he excitedly replied.

"Can I go, too?" Evie cried out.

"I'm sorry, honey. You'll have to wait till you are six years old," Suelena answered.

"Is that a long time?" the little girl asked.

Suelena held up two fingers. "This many years."

"You can help me in the kitchen." Mema tried to contribute in smoothing over the conversation. "I'm going to make cookies today and I really could use your help."

"Okay." Evie appeared satisfied with the suggestion. She did enjoy her new Mema.

"We'd better be on our way or we'll be late for school. Does Charlie have a jacket?" Suelena asked with concern.

"Not yet, but I'm working on one. We'll wrap this blanket around him for today, so he doesn't get cold or wet," Bonnie stated.

Soon Paul dropped off the two passengers at the school house, and waved good-bye. "I'll pick you both up after school," he called out.

Valora finished cleaning up after the breakfast meal, then tackled the rest of the house. Afterwards she started peeling and coring apples for pies and making apple butter from the freshly harvested basket of fruit Tom had brought in from their small orchard.

Gruffy, the bear, became more and more restless in the small pen that had been created just for him. It was obvious he missed the brother cub he yearned to play with. Valora still

139

hoped the inclement weather would clear up for the picnic they planned for Saturday. Letting the bear go free became uppermost on her mind now, since she had made the decision to release the pet. She could only trust and breathe a prayer for the children to accept the idea.

Caught up in her dreamland, the day sailed by rather rapidly. She was only brought back to reality after hearing Suelena's voice calling her name outside, "Valora! Valora! Hurry! Come see what's out here."

Valora quickly untied her apron, tossing it on the table, anxious to find out what all the ruckus was about. When she opened the door, she blurted, "Oh, it's beautiful!" Her hands clasped over her mouth.

There, near the front porch, sat Paul and Suelena in the most magnificent black carriage she had ever seen. The enormous buggy contained a well padded two-seater facing the horses pulling the vehicle. Behind was an exact two-seater situated in the opposite direction, and another facing towards the front. It would seat six people very comfortably. A black canopy with an ornamental fringe bordering the edge covered the passengers. "How impressive!" she said.

"May I sit in it? Is the carriage ours?" she kept asking questions.

"Yep. Come on. Let's all go for a ride," Paul urged Valora and the rest of the family who had joined them by now.

They all climbed into the carriage and sat down on the comfortable leather cushioned seats. Valora ran her hand over the smooth, black cushions and inspected the excellent workmanship, as the team of horses pulled the carrier ever so smoothly over the well-traveled roadway leading towards town. She felt like a queen riding in such luxury.

"Isn't it grand?" Suelena exclaimed, entranced with delight.

Joel's pleasure with the carriage was apparent. The admirable condition of the used carriage amazed him. Paul explained that the family they purchased it from was new in the area and hadn't owned it for very long. And although they didn't really want to part with the vehicle, they were going through some rough financial times and needed the money worse than they needed the carriage.

"It's getting dinner time. We'd better head back home," Joel finally stated. "We hope you girls will enjoy our new transportation, and please feel free to use it anytime."

Sunshine came peeping through the lace curtains, waking up Valora the following morning. She slowly opened her eyes, then stretched. All of a sudden it dawned on her . . . the sun could actually shine. This thrilled her, as she jumped out of bed and ran to the window, opening it long enough to capture a breath of fresh invigorating air. It took her but a brief moment to dress and hurry into the kitchen. However, this time she found Suelena already cooking the morning meal.

"Good morning. Isn't it a glorious day?" Suelena announced. "I woke early. When I looked outside, I saw a brilliant rainbow spreading across the sky. It seemed like our own private rainbow, appearing to touch the barn on one end and the other aimed in the direction of town. We're going to have an exceptional day. I just know it."

"Greetings, dear ladies." Joel came into the room. "And what enticing food do I smell for breakfast?"

"Pancakes, Valora's homemade strawberry and blackberry syrups, eggs, bacon and coffee," Suelena answered the older man, while pouring him a cup of the hot beverage she knew he came in for.

"Sounds good enough to eat!" Paul grinned as he entered the kitchen.

Tom already sat at the table with fork in one hand and a

knife in the other. "I'm starved. Where's the food?" he hollered teasingly.

"I'm going to ride into town with you again, Suelena. I need to show you a few pointers, so you will be able to take the carriage home by yourself."

"But it's so big!" Suelena interrupted Paul. "I'll never be able to handle it by myself."

"Sure you can. That's why we bought it. So you and Valora will be better protected from the weather," Paul assured her. "And besides, I need to pick up the buckboard and the other team of horses that I left behind. I'll leave the carriage at the stable for you."

"You men are really terrific and so thoughtful. We feel truly blessed." Valora spoke with gratitude in her voice and a smile on her lips.

"Ain't nothing, ma'am." Tom winked at her. "We just want another one of your berry pies for dinner tonight, that's all."

"You'll have it," she gracefully curtsied and winked back.

After Joel and Tom set out for their respective chores and Paul and Suelena started for town, Valora began planning the picnic in her mind for the next day, while starting to make crust for the berry pies. *By tomorrow the sun's warmth should dry the ground well enough to have an enjoyable day,* she thought. She hadn't been to the Judsons' all week, but Sarah and Valora had already discussed what foods to take and what time to meet together.

Saturday arrived with another sunny entrance, declaring a golden autumn morning. The vividly painted leaves in all their glory began to float down gracefully from sturdy tree branches surrounding the house. Although delightful, there was a slight chill to the light breeze. The sparkling dew gradually evaporated. What fun, as well as a challenge to anticipate the picnic Valora wanted so much to turn out just right. This was a day she wished for the children to remember as an exciting experience, not an unhappy one.

Following breakfast clean-up, Valora and Suelena loaded the new carriage with the food, eating utensils, blankets and other necessities. A desire rose up in Suelena hoping something would happen today to help change the attitude of David, the young twin. She had taken care to encourage him the past week, but as yet, saw no noticeable difference in his attitude.

With the carriage ready and Gruffy tied to the side with a long rope, the girls waved their good-byes and started for the Judsons to pick up Sarah and the four youngsters. After arriving at their neighbor's abode, they found the children anxiously watching for them to come. At first they didn't recognize Valora in the new carriage, then they noticed the bear lumbering along behind the vehicle and ran to greet them.

"Hi, Miss Valora. Is that yours?" One of the children couldn't help but ask, so excited. She nodded her head yes and smiled.

"Do we get to ride in the new carriage?"

"It's so big!"

"Can I ride up front?"

"Oh," someone giggled. "There's Gruffy." The animal showed equal elation in seeing his playmates.

Everyone was so excited and began asking questions all at once. "First, I want to introduce you to my sister, Suelena." Valora went through all the names: Susie, Kaye, David and Daniel, and of course, Sarah. The boys' faces showed surprise when they found out their school teacher was also Valora's sister. The girls shyly expressed their pleasure to meet her.

Suelena noticed that David had become a little shy, and suggested, "Why don't you boys sit up front with me? And Valora, why don't you sit back with Sarah and the girls?"

"That's a great idea." Valora helped Susie and Kaye into the carriage, while Sara helped her brothers up with Suelena. They loaded Sarah's contribution to the outing and soon were on their way.

The winding road led them by lush fields of green with a variety of fall wild flowers blending their colors here and there. They passed tall, stately firs, crossed over a bridge covering a clear stream, where they spotted a beaver busily building a dam in the distance. Now and then migrating birds flew overhead, flying south in the usual form of a "V," while the company of picnickers made their way over one rolling hill and another. After a short time the vibrant blue Bear Lake, the name given the expanse of water after discovering "their" bears, could be seen afar off in the background.

"Look for a shady spot to lay our blankets," Suelena called out.

"Over there by the big maple tree along the lake. That's where we came before," Daniel cried out.

The young women helped the girls out of the carriage. The boys had already jumped out. The restless bear was untied. The quilted blankets were spread under the huge maple. A gray squirrel scampered down the tree chattering, as if scolding them for the intrusion of his domain. Gruffy followed the children scurrying down to the lake. The frolicsome animal plunged in, splashing his playmates with icy water. They yelled and giggled and the boys splashed him back. The girls began turning cartwheels in the carpet of grass, while the boys skipped rocks across the lake, being extra careful not to hit the bear.

In the meantime, while setting out the luncheon of a variety of salads, sandwiches, Sarah's fried chicken, along with cupcakes and cookies, the preparation provided an opportunity for Suelena and Sarah to get to know each other.

After a while the youngsters became tired and expressed

how starved their tummies felt. Warm rays shining through the tree limbs from the bright sun overhead supplied enjoyment. Fresh air along with the tranquil setting, after being cooped up in a house for several days, was sublimely appreciated. Everyone had a healthy appetite and each of the children received permission to feed Gruffy whatever he chose to eat from the menu. Eventually, Valora set out a small jar of honey for the pet to enjoy for this occasion.

He looked so whimsical, sitting on his haunches, holding the jar between his paws while licking out the honey. A growl of approval could be heard now and then, as if he should let everyone know how much he treasured such a special treat. Soon the jar was empty. He went looking for more . . . first to one person, then another. The children started hollering, "Stay away from me. You're messy!" And ran off a ways . . . with Gruffy close at their heels, thoroughly amusing the women with his antics.

After repacking the leftover food into the carriage, Sarah called out, "Shall we go for a *short* hike?"

"Yesss!" sounded the penetrating response.

"We must stay close by each other. Remember what happened last time we came here!" Valora didn't really have to remind them.

They found what looked similar to a path, probably made by wild animals, leading away from the lake. The trail became very rugged, full of chug holes, boulders, fallen logs to climb over and thick bushes and tall grass to surge through. Gruffy appeared so natural in these surroundings, roaming free, inspecting logs while foraging for more food. Suddenly he spied something in a tree and in no time clambered up near the top.

"Shh." Suelena put her finger to her lips and whispered, "Look over towards the clearing. Can you see two deer, a doe and her fawn, pausing by that grove of trees?"

A short distance up the trail David heard a whimpering

sound and went to investigate. He carefully followed the direction of the whine and discovered a baby wolf. One of its legs had been caught between two large, jagged rocks. In the animal's struggle for freedom, his leg appeared to be injured. The little boy called to the group to help with the rescue.

"Be careful, David. He might bite you," Sarah warned, but the small animal seemed to sense the concern of the lad.

With plenty of strength from each of the women, one of the bulky rocks finally moved just enough to release the paw. Valora said it looked to be broken.

David gently picked up the wounded whelp and cuddled him to his chest, whispering softly to the little animal, "Don't worry, fella, I'll fix you up." The young pup was trembling, but licked the boy's face. He chuckled, then asked his older sister, "Do we have any rags I can use to make a splint?"

"I think we can find something back with the picnic supplies. Are we all ready to make the trek back to the carriage?" Sarah asked.

Everyone felt concern for the injured animal and agreed, as they made their way back to the horses and carriage. Valora located a dish towel she had used to wrap sandwiches in. She tore it into strips, while David found a couple fairly flat sticks. He placed them on either side of the broken leg, and wrapped the strips of cloth around the leg protected by the sticks, tying them carefully so as not to hurt his new little friend.

"My, you did such a good job," Suelena complimented him. "Maybe you'll make a fine veterinarian someday."

"What's that?" he asked.

"It's a person who helps heal injuries and diseases of animals," she explained simply.

"Yes. That's what I wanna be when I grow up. I love animals."

"You know, that means it would be necessary to get good grades in school and learn all you can about how to treat animals. Then one day you would need to go to a special school for veterinarians to learn about the different kinds of animal diseases, their bone structure and such," Suelena kept encouraging him.

He thought for a moment, then said, "Hmm, I guess I could do that."

"Whatcha going to name him?" Susie wanted to know.

"I think I'll call him Rocky, 'cause I found him in the rocks."

"That's a perfect name," Valora agreed.

"May I hold him for a while? I promise I'll be very careful," Daniel pleaded.

"Oh, all right, but be very careful." He wasn't quite ready to give him up yet, but laid the pup gently in his brother's arms. "I sure hope Pa will let me keep him," David said somewhat concerned, since his father wouldn't let them keep the bears.

"Well, with him being injured and a whole lot smaller than the bears, I believe Pa will," Sarah assured him, but not altogether sure herself. "You must remember to promise you'll take care of him. You know, feeding and cleaning up after him."

"I will. We're already pals," David quickly agreed.

Gruffy still sat propped up in the tree relishing in the beehive he had found, as they passed by where they had last seen him. Angry bees were buzzing around his head, but they didn't seem to deter the bear a bit.

"This is probably the perfect time to say good-bye to Gruffy, while he's enjoying his newfound freedom," Valora suggested. "It seems to me that he will do just fine here in the wild. Don't you think?"

"Bye, Gruffy," the children called and waved to their friend, their voices sounding not quite sure they agreed with Valora. He looked their way for a second, then went back to the business of enjoying the savory treat. Tears fell down their solemn faces, as well as from Valora's eyes, while tearing at her heart as they left their pet behind. She knew the decision was best for all concerned, and picked up the pace as they found their way back to the waiting carriage and horses.

The day hadn't turned out quite like she had perceived, but a rather nice trade . . . a wolf for a bear. At least Rocky wouldn't eat as much. She meditated on these thoughts filling her heart, while they rode back in the direction of their respective homes, absorbed in the somberness of the occasion.

David held his new pet now. Susie and Kaye sat on the floor of the carriage at their brother's feet, petting the young, wild animal. Suddenly Rocky let out a big yawn. He licked the girls' faces . . . they giggled. The pup looked up into his new master's face, curled up to him snugly and went immediately to sleep in apparent contentment.

Thirteen

Trees, stark and bare, envisioned no match for the vivid glow of autumn that had faded and could have left a dreary landscape, but for the magnificence of evergreens: western hemlock, cedar, spruce and firs. With each day comes a new beginning, with each new year a time to reflect over the old. Many changes can take place in such a short span of time. With the holidays drawing near, Valora started to focus her thoughts on the day of Thanksgiving, recalling earlier celebrations.

Memories of times past can afford us with great pleasures mixed in with sensitive emotions. Everyone she had come to care for these several months had experienced a loss of a loved one. The Bible teaches we should be thankful in all things, as we draw on the strength of God who is the compass of our path.

For Valora, it was difficult to imagine being thankful for some things, like the death of the ones who had given her earthly life . . . her loving parents. Still, she could see how miraculously God had guided her to the McCalister family, even the day of their loss of a wife and mother. They had come to fill her void, as per chance she and her sister may have been a help for them. No one can ever take the place of another; nevertheless, a new love can grow and branch out into blossoms that can touch a heart and magnify the soul. God can take a pitiful life and turn it into a spiritual dignity, if we would only surrender to His will. Why are we so afraid to let go and let

God make us what He wants us to be? Why do we maneuver our minds into thinking, if we go God's way it must be opposite of what we could ever enjoy? Of course we're not promised a bed of roses without thorns, even if we yield to our Creator's guidance. However, God promised His strength, His comfort and His everlasting love, if we will submit to His direction and rely on Him to carry us through the troubled times that do come our way.

In ancient times many peoples of the world held special festivals in autumn to give thanks for their good harvests. Most pilgrims who had come to America probably knew some form of thanksgiving in their homelands and encouraged the transplanting of such a special custom in our great land.

Valora learned earlier, when reading history books that the first day of Thanksgiving in America was held in the early 1600s by the colonists claiming the new land. Many lives had been lost en route, while sailing the treacherous waters of the Atlantic, and those who survived the voyage gave thanks to God for their survival.

Ever since 1863, Thanksgiving has been observed annually in America, usually the last or fourth Thursday of November; a specified time when farmers come together for a pause to give thanks and gratitude to God for their bountiful harvests. The Bible even teaches that Moses urged his people not to forget their God, who miraculously led them out of slavery into a land they would call their own.

Jesus reminds us, if God takes care of the tiny sparrow, how much more He will take care of His children. In the Lord's Prayer He states, we are to ask daily for our food. Not that God won't supply our needs, nevertheless, He wants us to remember every day to talk to the one who is the provider of His people, and make Him a part of our daily lives.

As Valora contemplated this joyous occasion, Joel came

into the kitchen and noticed her deep in thought. "And what might our lovely lady be conjuring up in your mind this day?"

"If it would be all right with you, Papa Mack, I'd like to plan a special dinner and try to make this Thanksgiving a very memorable event."

"Did you have something in mind?"

"I know it's probably a lot to ask, even so, I would like to invite the Judson family, the sheriff, Bonnie and her children, and maybe even Doctor and Mrs. Rider for dinner this Thanksgiving. It will be the first time for us to be all together."

"Hmm. I believe that's an excellent suggestion. We can fix up some makeshift tables and benches and set them on into the living room. Yes, I like the idea. It will mean extra work for you though."

"I'm sure Suelena, Sarah, and I can plan the meal together and share in the preparation. And I would love to do it. I'll talk to Suelena this evening and Sarah tomorrow." She couldn't hold back her enthusiasm.

"To be honest with you," Joel admitted, "I wasn't really looking forward to the holidays this year. You and your sister have been a real blessing to our family, Valora. I couldn't have prayed for a lovelier daughter, and now I feel I have two." He gave her a hug. They both felt a definite tenderness for one another.

Preparations were soon underway. Sarah and her family indicated their delight with the invitation to join their beloved friends for the holiday. Mr. Judson was raising turkeys for the big day and said he'd fatten them up real good. Bonnie exhibited real pleasure, too, but declined the offer. Mrs. Rider had already asked the sheriff, along with Bonnie and her children, to spend Thanksgiving with them and evidenced excitement about their plans. She knew holidays can be so lonely for those without family or friends to share them with. Everyone who

151

meant so much to Valora would be taken care of; that was really her desire.

The Saturday before Thanksgiving Mark came sauntering in from college with a big grin on his handsome face, just as the family sat down for the evening meal. "Looks like I timed it just right," he said.

Joel got up from his chair at the head of the table and gave his youngest son a fatherly welcome, "It's so good to have you home, Mark. How've you been? You look hungry. I believe you have lost weight."

"I've missed Valora's great cooking. " He gave her a wink, then he noticed Suelena. "Well, well. Looks like we have a guest."

"Oh, please meet my sister, Suelena. She now lives here with us, too." Valora introduced the two of them.

"I've been staying in your room, but I'll gladly give it up to you," Suelena said modestly. "Valora and I'll share her bedroom while you're home. Please excuse some of my clothes. Papa Mack said you could share with Tom or Paul's room, but I don't want you to have to do that."

"Hey, I don't mind . . . unless they snore!" They all laughed at his teasing.

"No, please, it will be fun sharing a room with my sister," she quickly added.

"Come, sit down and eat with us." Joel pulled out a chair.

"Let me wash up and I'll be right back. After dinner I want to go by and see the Judsons this evening. Although I probably should wait and see them in church tomorrow."

"You mean Sarah?" Paul bantered with him.

"Yeh, I guess I am rather eager to see Sarah," he said. "I really haven't been very faithful about writing letters to her."

"She's anxious to see you. You'd better go over tonight, or she'll never forgive you!" Valora encouraged him.

When the big day arrived, Valora and Suelena rose early to stuff dressing into the turkeys Mr. Judson had insisted they accept. Sarah was also preparing another one. The girls previously baked pies of pumpkin, apple and homemade mincemeat, with real meat, the day before. Fresh vegetables of white and sweet potatoes, green beans and corn, which had been canned from the summer garden, and a fruit salad of apples, peaches and different kinds of berries from their land were waiting to perform their delight in the menu.

The men busily set at moving and arranging furniture to give them more room for the makeshift tables and benches they had crafted. Eventually, the structures were covered with tablecloths, colorful napkins and the best dishes and utensils. Bouquets of brilliantly hued chrysanthemums found a place at each end of the long extended table, candles surrounded each vase. Suelena had even created turkey name plates for every person who would be attending. The setting looked elegant. By the time the guests arrived, the room had transformed into a festive atmosphere of pleasantries and delicious aromas.

Along with the turkey and dressing, Sarah brought deviled eggs, a salad and she had found and baked her mother's favorite recipe for applesauce cake to add to the banquet. Her father, Luke, brought with him a jovial mood along with his fiddle. The children beamed with excitement and overflowed with chatter.

Little David had secretly tried to conceal Rocky, his pet wolf, under his coat. But the pup was too big. So instead, David hid him under the seat in the buckboard until they arrived at the McCalister ranch. Although his father scolded him, Joel convinced his friend to let the boy bring the pup on in the house. He had only heard about the pet and wanted to see him. Much of the boy's time lately included training the animal in discipline. Valora was amazed at how well he followed David's instructions, and also the puppy's growth. He was quite playful and trailed his young master wherever he went. When the time came to gather around the table and partake in the joyous occasion of this feast day, Rocky found his place at David's feet under the table.

Watching each one locate their name plates on the table became amusing. Joel asked the Lord's blessings on the meal and thanked Him for the provisions and health He had granted them. A warmth of friendship filled the home. Everyone ate too much of the scrumptious meal, while sharing in conversation.

After clearing the table and dishes put away, Valora asked Tom to bring in a large tub filled with bright red apples grown in their orchard. She filled it with water, then summoned the youngsters to bob for apples with their arms placed behind their backs. The children became tickled each time one would come up out of the water, dripping wet from trying to catch an apple in their mouths, while racing to see which one could outdo the other. Little Kaye, the youngest, nearly fell into the tub, as she came up out of the water sputtering, while struggling to catch her treasure.

Sometime later Joel called the clan together after each child had their turn bobbing for apples. A brisk fire set off a glow from the fireplace, making the room feel cozy on this chilly day. The adults found a chair or sat on the large couch. The smaller children placed themselves on the floor eager to find out what would come next.

Joel read from Psalm 100 in the Bible, then said, "In the Old Testament days of the Bible the sacrifice of thanksgiving was an offering of something very valuable to its owner. The gift amounted to being the finest they possessed. These were voluntary offerings, not required or given at a stated time of the year like we are observing today. They instead were presented when the people felt especially thankful to the Lord.

"Our country was established by people who came

154

searching for religious freedom. They became known as Pilgrims who migrated to Massachusetts and formed the Plymouth Colony over two hundred years ago. These people gave thanks to God for the new land they had found and the good crops they harvested their first year. This has become a memorable custom in our country ever since. Psalm 107:1 reads, 'O give thanks unto the Lord, for He is good: for His mercy endureth forever.' (KJV)

"I'd like each of us to take time to think about one thing we are thankful for," he suggested.

"I'm thankful for Rocky," David went first.

"I'm thankful for good friends that would open up their home to us on this very special day of Thanksgiving," Luke Judson replied.

Each one took their turn giving thanks, and last Joel imparted, "Let's remember that giving thanks is more than being thankful for material things. We should be thankful for those, too, but for life, health, family and friends. These precious gifts are really what brings about an importance to our lives.

"I remember when our first house burned to the ground . . . how devastated I felt. Then I looked at my wife and boys and thanked God they had been spared. We could build another house, as well as furniture. The precious mementos could not be replaced, but it was the lives that remained which was more meaningful than all those 'things.'

"It was you, my dear friend, Luke, and our other neighbors who came to our rescue. You shared your home with us until we could rebuild, and then you helped us construct this fine house; a home more grand than the first. It's not just the construction of a lovely place to live, but the building of relationships. The giving of oneself for the good of someone else, that's the true harvest that instills the heart to warming.

"On the way over here today, I know you went by the widow lady, Mrs. Smalley's, and took her a turkey and the trimmings. This is the true spirit of Thanksgiving. Through the gift of giving something of ourselves to someone else, we receive the most precious gifts ... friendship, love and self-worth.

"So, today, a day of Thanksgiving, I would like to offer a prayer," each one bowed their head, "I thank the Lord this day for my sons, my two 'adopted' daughters, and dear friends who make my life meaningful. May God enrich our lives the rest of this year and into the next. May we grow in His love and service to others. Amen.

"Now, it's time for some merriment. Luke, where's that fiddle? Tom, your harmonica? It's too bad we don't have someone to play Mattie's piano."

"Valora plays the piano beautifully," Suelena said.

"And Suelena sings," Valora grinned at her sister.

"You girls are full of surprises," Joel sounded amazed.

Mark had to head back to Seattle for college on the following Sunday afternoon, causing a void in hearts of his family and friends.

A few days after the holiday of feasts, Valora rode with Suelena into Cascadia to stock up on provisions for the family. Although the sky shown overcast, the weather felt mild for the time of year. After letting Suelena off at the school house and upon entering town, Valora waved at some of the familiar acquaintances she had previously befriended, but her waves went unnoticed. While in the general store, Mrs. Jones took care of her needs, then asked Jake to take over for her.

"Valora, I hope you consider me a friend. Please understand what I'm going to say is certainly not my opinion in the least, nevertheless I feel you need to be told."

"There's been some people talking, and I dislike very much what they are saying." She hesitated, not quite knowing exactly what words to form. "Some people are expressing some unkind and unjust opinions . . . well . . . some are saying it's not right for two young unmarried women to live in the same house with four unmarried men." She finally expressed herself with embarrassment.

"What! Oh, my! Surely they don't think . . . but everyone in this area knows, and I thought respected Joel McCalister and his sons. We're in church nearly every Sunday, unless illness or out of town. Oh, dear!" Valora felt completely flabbergasted.

"Well, with Suelena being a teacher and all . . . I'm just worried, Valora. The tongue can be very cruel. 'And you know, schoolmarms should be unmarried and above reproach,' as one lady put it . . . I mean woman, she's certainly not acting like a lady."

"Thank you, Annie, for telling me, even though it's painful news. I'm glad you are friend enough to let me know. I'd best be getting on home now. I've got some thinking to do." Valora hugged her friend. Both women were overcome with intense emotions.

Once you've climbed a mountain, sooner or later you have to go down into the valley. Up on a mountaintop it seems nothing ever could be contrary to principled conduct. The cares of the world can disappear in your imagination and the mind clears. It's a good time to take inventory of your life, to set goals and challenges. Now, this was going to be a real contention to wrestle with. Not one she would enjoy; a character builder just the same. Valora harbored both emotions of betrayal and anguish, not only for herself, but for the ones she loved so deeply as well. She asked God to guide her thoughts and give her wisdom.

At the supper table everyone except Valora expressed their usual talkative selves, relating the affairs of the day. Joel perceived Valora not to be her normal chattery person and asked, "Is something bothering you, Valora?"

Valora released a deep sigh. She had been wondering all day how to tell her family. "There's been talk around town . . ." She didn't want to say the words . . . after a pause, she added, . . . "Gossip . . . about two young unmarried women sharing a home with four unmarried men."

Suelena gasped.

Joel's eyes became enormous. Valora had never seen Papa Mack so enraged. He was really trying very hard to contain himself; except he looked as if he might explode at any minute. Then he hit the table with his fist, causing even the dishes on the table to jump. Finally, he asked, "Who told you this?"

"Annie Jones at the store. She felt we should know what's being said, and appeared very sensitive to our feelings."

"Yes, Annie's been a good friend through the years. I'm convinced she would not be the one to spread such nonsense," Joel agreed.

"Somehow we need to nip this in the bud, Pa." Tom could not control his agitated composure any longer.

"Why do people always have to think the worst about others?" Paul asked with disgust in his voice.

"Not everyone does, thank God. A lot is just foolish jealousy or guilt. But, we're not going to let this get us down. We'll handle it," Papa Mack replied, sounding confident.

The next morning Joel rode into town, still feeling glum. After being gone all morning, when he entered the house the expression on his face looked much more pleasant.

Sunday morning arrived with a roar of thunder and a flash of lightning striking across the dark, gray sky. Each one climbed on board the carriage, Joel had waiting out the back door, thankful for the covering of the canopy. The girls sat close together to stay warm, wrapped in a blanket. Tom and Paul sat opposite them, while Joel urged the team of horses on towards town and church. The trip to Cascadia remained one of silence.

In spite of the inclement weather, the church was crammed full of people. Valora recognized the ones who had ignored her earlier in the week with a forced smile. The Riders, Bonnie and her children, the Judson family, Annie Jones, even Sheriff Randal, who normally didn't attend services, all nodded their hellos. When the McCalisters and the girls entered, the congregation suddenly became quiet. All eyes were trained on them, as they found a pew and squeezed in behind the Judsons.

Interestingly enough the pastor directed his sermon from the Book of James, chapter three, where the brother of Jesus speaks about the tongue. How a small bit in a horse's mouth can be used to train the animal to obey its master and turn his whole body in the direction that person is wanting the horse to go. Or another example may be how the very small helm of a great ship can be used to turn a ship about. Even though the tongue is only a small member of our body parts, out of the same mouth that houses it can come blessings and cursing. The tongue can be full of deadly poison, and can become unruly if not tamed. James goes on to say, "My brethren, these things ought not to be."

And the pastor said, "My brothers and sisters of this congregation, this ought not to be. It has been brought to my attention that there has been some talking going on . . . some poison being spread. Again, my brothers and sisters, this ought not to be. James, chapter one verse twelve states, 'Blessed is the man that endureth temptation: for when he is tried, he shall receive the crown of life, which the Lord had promised to them that love Him.'

"We have a family present today that have been treated rather poorly in our community as of late. Joel McCalister has proven himself to be an upright, God- fearing man for many years in this fair settlement. And I might add, so have his sons, and the two sisters . . . orphans . . . he has given a home to this past year. At the close of our service I'm going to ask this family to stand at the back of the sanctuary. As you exit God's house today, if there are any among you that may need to make an apology to this family, you will have the opportunity to do so at that time. Now let us sing, 'What a Friend We Have in Jesus.' "

At the close of the service, as the congregation made their way out the double doors of the church building, the faces portrayed shame-filled hearts. Everyone in attendance shook the hands of Joel, his sons, Valora and Suelena. Some gave hugs and whispered their expressions of regret, others had tears in their eyes. Love can only be restored when people own up to their wrongs and ask for forgiveness, not only to those who have been wrongfully treated, but to God, the only one who can really forgive our sins.

Peace was restored in the little community church in Cascadia that day. And no more remained to be said of the rumors that had prompted the pastor's message.

Fourteen

Looking out her bedroom window at the snow-clad mountains in the distance, Valora sensed the hushing sounds of the frosted evergreens in the primeval forest amidst unadorned limbs of maple and oak trees. She found such pleasure in anticipating the joys and wonderment of the Christmas season. Singing the beautiful songs, decorating the house with fresh smelling garlands and candles, and creating homemade ornaments out of flour and salt to hang on the tree. All these things commandeered their role in the festivity she loved about this holiday season. To experience the same warm feeling of satisfaction she had felt on Thanksgiving, and make memories that would linger on and be treasured for generations filled her desire.

Some of the most precious impressions remembered were the almost magical, carefree days of her childhood. Her father always wanted to be the one to inspect the decorated tree to see if it needed just one more ornament here or there, and place the bright shining star on the highest bough to add that finishing touch. Mama's skill of expertise truly shined in making their home a showplace with her artistic talent in arranging dried flowers with boughs and bows, pine cones and wreathes.

Valora decided to sew everyone a large stocking, personalizing them with names for each one in the family to hang on the mantle above the fireplace. She hoped, between Suelena and herself, they could remember their mother's fruit cake and fudge recipes they had helped make, as well as a variety of Christmas cookies that invariably were devoured so quickly.

That evening while sitting around the table for the last meal of the day, Tom mentioned hearing about a hayride for carolers being planned for the coming weekend.

"Oh, let's go," Valora and Suelena said simultaneously.

"I thought you girls might like the idea. How about you, Paul and Pa? Mark might be home in time, too."

"Sure, why not," Paul agreed.

Papa Mack didn't appear so thrilled with the notion, and decided to give it some thought; not wanting to put a damper on the enthusiastic response from the girls.

When light peeked through the window on Saturday morning, Valora lazily opened her eyes and stretched, then slowly proceeded to rise from her warm, comfortable bed. She peered out the window to check on the weather. To her delight sparkling, white flakes were floating quietly to the ground. Winter's snowy face turned the scenery into a dreamy fairyland. The long, fir branches had captured the crystallized flakes until they bowed as if in silent prayer. Icicles had already begun to form on the eaves of the house. A gentle ambience cast its spell by joining in the inspiration of the holiday spirit, causing one to thank God for another of His priceless gifts.

Valora quickly put on her clothes, went to the kitchen and started a fire in the cook stove, which soon sent off a soothing, inviting warmth to the chamber. Suelena presently entered the room yawning.

Suelena pulled back the lacy white curtain to glance out the window, releasing a squeal of delight, "Snow! Isn't it beautiful? What a glorious day. Won't it be perfect for the hayride tonight?"

The men came ambling in one by one ready to partake of

the frying eggs on the stove, bacon and freshly baked biscuits and gravy. "Looks like winter has set in," Tom kissed Valora on the top of her head, grabbing a strip of bacon at the same time.

"A white Christmas. Wouldn't that be just perfect?" she remarked.

"Don't get your hopes up too much. Snow doesn't stay around here that long," Joel reminded her.

"I'm going to hope for it just the same," Suelena said.

It snowed off and on all day, maybe twelve inches at the most. The men had taken the wheels off the carriage and attached large runners like skis in their place, turning the carriage into a sleigh. They all piled in, even Joel, and went gliding off towards town chattering and laughing all the way. A dainty flake still fell now and then, as they slid ever so smoothly over the road adorned in glistening snow. The crisp air tantalized their lungs. The foliage and dense undergrowth of the forest sparkled with a covering of white, creating a special touch of wonderment and serenity.

As they came upon the steepled structure, a crowd began to congregate around the steps of the well-kept church building, too many for one vehicle. Fortunately several had anticipated this might happen and brought their wagons full of hay.

The families were split up, so that all four wagons had members from each family. Valora felt pleased that she and Tom rode in the same wagon with Sarah and Mark, who had come in from college earlier in the day. Suelena, Paul, Sheriff Randal and Bonnie and her family rode on another buckboard. Joel found Luke Judson and Annie Jones and joined with their team. Someone decided the wagons should depart in different directions, then meet back at the church building for hot apple cider or hot chocolate, when finished caroling. The Riders and those who eagerly relinquished their place to the younger members for the ride, accepted the responsibility of being in charge of refreshments.

A full moon shone bright, enhancing the beauty with eternally snow-clad Mt. Rainier for a background. The midnight sky showed off the star-studded heavens, as the horses pulled the hay-laden wagons full of exuberant carolers over the white covered ground, singing *It Came Upon the Midnight Clear; Good Christian Men, Rejoice; Away in a Manger,* and more lovely songs to fill hearts and souls for this season of rejoicing in music and merrymaking.

When all sung out, the groups made their trek back to the chapel, where they found hot beverages waiting to warm up their chilled bodies along with Christmas snacks and goodies. Each took part in a time of fellowship and sharing how hearts had been stirred with the true meaning of Christmas as they caroled. The evening affair came to a close with everyone joining in singing the beloved, *Silent Night, Holy Night.*

"Don't forget church services tomorrow." The pastor couldn't miss the opportunity to remind everyone before they went their separate ways.

"What a wonder filled evening," Valora remarked, as their carriage took them in the direction of home. "It made me feel so good inside, when we'd stop at people's homes and sing the carols. Some of the folks I'd never seen before came to the windows or their front porches to join in or just smile with pleasure at being remembered."

"Those who give of themselves many times receive more satisfaction than those who are the recipients. Although once in a while we get to experience the joy of observing someone really touched and thankful," Joel reflected.

As the time drew closer to Christmas, Joel noticed both Valora and Suelena were spending more and more time in their respective bedrooms. He started to become concerned, wondering if something might be wrong between the two, or perhaps even the rest of the family. Finally, he couldn't contain himself and had to ask one of the girls.

Valora grinned, saying, "Now, Papa Mack, you aren't supposed to ask questions around Christmas."

Her response set at ease his troubled thoughts to his embarrassment. They both evidently had some kind of secret in progress pertaining to the holidays, which used up their time, but he missed the evenings together as a family. He felt pleased that Mark was home again for several days on a break from his schooling in Seattle, although he too spent much of his time over at the Judsons'.

A great extent of creative imagination went into decorating the house; the girls had really outdone themselves. Joel couldn't remember the home looking so exquisite, even when Mattie had been alive. Stockings that Valora had so artfully crafted hadn't been seen hung over the hearth since his sons were tykes. Baskets of pine cones and greenery of garlands decorated with bright red bows enlivened the rooms, bringing in the fragrance of freshness from the outdoors.

After Suelena arrived home from school the following day, everyone was ready to set out to locate two Christmas trees, one for the Judsons as well as the McCalisters. Mark had picked up Sarah in the Judsons' buckboard, providing plenty of room for all. And, so as not to break the family tradition, they went to the same special place where they had gone every year since Joel and Mattie moved to the Washington Territory.

The melting snow caused even more chug holes in the normally rugged road, as it climbed to a higher elevation. As they drew near their destination not far from the ranch, Valora could understand why they had chosen this particular spot to find the perfect tree; the location had a certain characteristic of its own. She imagined this place must be something like the rain forest in the Olympics she had heard so much about. Moss still hung gracefully from huge Douglas firs, while lacy green ferns covered the ground. Patches of frozen snow clung to some of the branches, making it a wintry fairyland.

"There's a beauty," Sarah called out. "If it's not too tall."

"We can always trim it to size, if the shape is what you like," Mark suggested.

"Uh, oh. The back looks rather sparse. Wait! There's a better one over by that huge tree. Yes. That's perfect," Sarah decided.

Mark cut it down before she could change her mind.

"Have you found one you like yet, Valora?" Tom asked.

"How about over there?" She climbed over a fallen log covered with moss, causing her to slip and fall. As she started to get up, she spied a small grayish coyote staring in her direction just a few feet away, then darted off into the woods. "He'd make a good friend for Rocky," she thought out loud, while Tom helped her up.

"Does everyone agree? Is this our perfect tree?" She asked, dwarfed by it's fullness and height.

"Excellent," Suelena proclaimed, satisfied.

"If both girls like it, the tree must be the right one," Joel agreed, and cut it down. Paul carried the tree carefully to the buckboard so as not to break any branches, then Tom helped him load the fir onto the wagon.

By the time they arrived back at the ranch, the sky had turned to dusk. The girls started supper, while the men fit the trees to their stands, and any needed trimming was performed. Following the meal, Sarah decided she best be getting on home. Mark helped with her coat then grabbed his and told everyone not to wait for him to help trim the tree. The girls brought out the ornaments they had made, while Joel lo-

166

cated the decorations from years past. They all set to work transposing the green fir into a dazzling, spangled elegance.

"Now we need some presents under the tree to make it perfect," Suelena exclaimed. "And I just happen to have some." She ran upstairs to her room where she had hid the gifts under Mark's bed before he came home for the holidays. Valora also went to her room. They both came back with brightly wrapped packages in their arms and placed them meticulously under the decorative tree.

"Uh, huh. So this is what you two have been up to. I guess that means we'll have to buy some presents, too," Tom teased.

"Naw. I think there's just enough to look good under there now," Paul joined in. "We don't want to spoil the supreme effect of excellence already achieved."

"I think it would look even more perfect with two more presents under there, don't you, Suelena?" Valora grinned.

"At least two," her sister carried on with the teasing.

By Christmas Eve, several more colorful gifts had found their place around the base of the tree. It was a busy day of activity finishing up last minute baking and projects before the Christmas Eve party being planned for that night took place. Suelena's winter break from teaching gave her more time to help Valora with the preparations. All sorts of candies, cookies, cakes and pies were arranged enticingly on the best china. Hot apple cider filled the entire house with an inviting, spicy aroma teasing the taste buds.

Soon the guests started arriving. Annie Jones brought her delicious prune cake. Mrs. Rider and Bonnie had prepared a lovely array of fancy frosted cookies. Sarah, with the help of her younger sisters, had made a variety of flavors of petite sandwiches in shapes of stars, balls, trees and animals. Sheriff Randal said he brought Bonnie and her family. Friends and family gathering together to share in the holiday spirit made this such a meaningful event, while remembering that the real celebration is to honor the birth of a special child, God's only Son. For this is the true reason such a glorious occasion has been set aside to enjoy, to show our thankfulness for God's greatest gift of love.

The men gathered in the living room by the toasty fire, while the ladies put the finishing touches on the display of foods, as well as catching up on the latest news. It wasn't long until the men joined in sharing timeless tales of the "good ole" days. The children found places on the floor surrounding the men, and soon became captivated by the astounding creative ability of such fine imaginations, as each man tried to outdo the other in sharing their yarns.

Doc Rider swore that his story was not a fabrication. He told about his relatives who had been attacked by some Cayuse Indians in an uprising over in the eastern Washington Territory near Yakima not too many years past. His folks had been some of the early pioneers to that area. While farming one day, their immediate neighbors saw a lot of smoke and flames shooting up to the sky in the distance, and decided they'd better head over in that direction to investigate. Upon their arrival they found the house nearly burned to the ground, mortally wounded bodies, and a woman's hand sticking out of the dirt; one of them happened to notice the hand move just a mite, hopefully attracting attention. As quickly as they could, they dug away the dirt and found Doc's aunt barely alive. Unfortunately, they found other members of the family dead from their injuries. On the other hand, Doc's aunt was nursed back to health and lived several more years to tell about her traumatic experience of being buried alive.

Mrs. Rider ended the narrative with more encouraging words, "Let's eat!"

Everyone assembled around the festive table. Joel asked for God's blessings on the hands that had prepared such succulent foods, the fine fellowship with dear friends and loved ones, and for all the many blessings God had bestowed upon each one.

After everyone finished stuffing themselves, Valora sat down at the piano and began to play music of the season. Gradually the members congregated around the musical instrument to put words to the sweet melodies. Even the smaller children sang some of the well known carols. Subsequently, Joel got out his well-worn Bible and called everyone together, as he read aloud the Christmas story in the Book of Luke, chapter two, verses one through twenty with sincere expression in his voice. Then he revived the scene of the Magi arriving with their significant gifts fit for a King.

"Is that why we give gifts today?" one of the children asked.

"I imagine that's how it started. But too many times we're so busy thinking of the presents, that we forget the real reason why we celebrate Christmas, the birth of Jesus, our Savior."

"Can I give Jesus a gift?" Susie wanted to know.

"The best gift you can give Jesus is to love Him with all of your heart, and maybe give something to someone who may be less fortunate that you are," Joel answered.

Time went by so swiftly. Soon everyone gathered their belongings and said good night, thanking their hosts for such a splendid evening.

Valora slept in warm content that night and awakened to a dreamy silent dawn. Peering out the window, as she usually did each morning, she found once more winter's treasure had unfolded the whisper of falling, white snowflakes. Snow, tipped evergreens glistened in white splendor. The ground shown lightly, covered snow, as large flakes whirled slowly downward in the cold, frosty air.

By the time she was dressed and in the kitchen Suelena had already set the table. "Isn't it wonderful? I hoped for a white Christmas, not really expecting one," Suelena revealed her delighted satisfaction.

The smile on Valora's face was answer enough, as she shook her head in agreement and helped in preparation of breakfast.

"Good morning, ladies." Joel gave each one a peck on the cheek. "Which one of you has been praying for snow again?" He grinned.

"I haven't exactly been praying for it, but I am pleased," Suelena answered him.

The other men filed in as Valora handed each a glass of freshly made eggnog, "a family Christmas tradition of the Dillon's," she pointed out. Then they all sat down to a table of pancakes and hot syrup, sausage and eggs.

Following the meal, the brothers said their gift would be to clean up the kitchen . . . but only on Christmas morning . . . then they led the young women to the living room. Valora said that could be a delightful McCalister tradition. The men just grinned. Joel had a welcome, roaring fire going in the massive fireplace, brightening up the decorated tree nearby.

As soon as the men completed their task in the kitchen, they joined their father and the sisters around the tree. Valora and Suelena were unanimously elected for the task of passing out the presents. One by one removal of the wrappings showed expressions of love. Each girl received a book of poems from Joel, a lovely imported scarf from Mark, and warm leather gloves from Paul. Suelena opened a small box containing a broach in the shape of an apple "for the teacher" from Tom.

Valora received a lovely emerald necklace encircled with pearls similar to the one she had found for her sister's reunion, knowing it would be a remembrance of their mother. Tom had been watching her as she unwrapped the small package. She became so filled with emotion for his thoughtfulness, that tears began to well up in her eyes, then she whispered, "Thank you so very much."

Suelena had hand-stitched each of the men a white shirt for church; and for her sister, a lovely fashionable dress in peach floral design. Valora had been learning the art of leather tooling from Mr. Judson, and crafted all the men and her sister an intricately designed belt with their names personalized on each one. For Mark and Suelena she styled a satchel with their names for carrying their books, for Joel and Paul a leather vest, and for Tom she designed a saddle bag with his name in fancy lettering.

"My, this must be why you girls spent so much time in your rooms here lately," Papa Mack said.

"We wanted to make each of you something special with our own hands," said Valora. "Each gift was truly sewn and crafted with love."

"And you certainly did," all the men agreed.

Soon the kitchen filled with the tantalizing fragrance of ham being prepared for the early afternoon meal. "Do we have time to go sledding before we eat?" Tom wandered into the kitchen and asked the girls.

Both young women squealed out a "Yes," and rushed to get their coats, boots, new gloves and scarves, and out the door they ran.

Paul threw a snowball, nearly hitting Suelena in the face. She stopped over and filled her gloves with snow and threw the packed ball at Paul, missing him completely. That just egged him on, as he started to chase her. In the meantime, Mark pulled a huge sled up a steep hill nearby with Valora and Tom close behind. Paul and Suelena finally ran in that direction, too. They climbed on board. Tom gave them a push and quickly jumped on behind the rest. The air produced a brisk cold wind, but they didn't mind, as they sped on down the slope laughing and hanging on tight to one another, changing directions with their bodies and in the swerving of the sled.

"Okay. You girls get to take the sled back up the hill," Paul teased, still sitting in the sled waiting for them to pull the sled up the hill with his body still in it.

Suelena picked up a handful of the white stuff and threw it his way; this time her aim hit her target perfectly, delivering the snowball right square in the back of his neck. Off she ran with Paul close behind. Several times they all trudged up the slippery hillside, only to swoop down again for a windy breathtaking ride. During the final ride down, the sled tipped over, dumping everybody into a snow bank. This helped the girls decide it was an opportune time to check on dinner. Soon they came back outside, convincing the guys how much fun it would be to shape a snowman. They rolled three huge balls of snow, stacked each one on top of the other, placing a carrot for a nose, rocks for the eyes and mouth, and a pitchfork in his round hand. To top it off Tom found an old cowboy hat to finish their masterpiece.

Later, after everyone had partaken of the savory Christmas meal with hearty satisfaction and good ole' enjoyment of eating scrumptious food, Valora and Suelena led the family in harmonizing Christmas music. Each one felt enraptured with the warmth of fellowship, as they ended the day sitting and gazing into the cozy, flickering fire in silence, while implanting precious memories in their heads.

Fifteen

The New Year rang in with a persistent clamor. Angry thunder roared out at the streaks of lightning clashing with strong winds, each trying to outdo the other with force. Limbs of trees were strewn all over, as they assumed their place of rest upon the soggy ground. One huge Douglas fir had fallen across the road, which led into town. Some of the neighbor's trees had smashed into the roofs of their barns. By the end of the day, the troubled sky gave way to a serene calm of almost whispering evergreens, as if to say, "Now I have your attention. Make good use of this new year God has granted to you . . . My creation."

What lies ahead in 1877?

The first day of a new year can be just another ordinary day, or a time for setting goals. The latter choice is the one Joel had always encouraged his family to participate in. He felt goals should be attainable, yet an incentive for challenges, a stimulus for motivation and growth.

Valora didn't exactly know what she wanted to happen in her life this year. She had dreams, but felt content running the household chores of the McCalister family. It was apparent that Suelena found satisfaction in her teaching position. She talked a lot about the children and how noticeably the twin, David, had made progress in changing his attitude and shown more interest in school. What else could they really desire? This family that had taken them in when they had no place to go seemed to need them, too.

173

Several days after the stormy winds had blown the area, the welcome sun finally broke out of its hiding place, winding its way through puffy clouds of gray, surrounding the valley with a freshness permeating the air. With her housework accomplished and preparations for dinner underway, Valora decided to take a walk through the wintry woods of leafless trees scattered amongst evergreens. She put on her dark, blue, winter coat, warm gloves, and wrapped the lovely scarf around her auburn hair, tying it snugly around her throat, enjoying the gifts she had received. She stepped out into a sharp cold refreshing breeze.

She hadn't gone very far when Tom called out for her to wait up. After pausing long enough for him to catch up, he asked if she would mind if he walked along with her. Pleased to have his company, they strolled hand in hand not saying a word, enjoying the peaceful time alone, except for the cheerful note of a bird now and then. Eventually, they came upon a clear, blue pond of shimmering water, where they found a fallen log to sit upon.

"It's so good to get outside for a little while." Valora broke the spell of silence, her head raised up toward the heavens, her eyes closed as she breathed in the fresh air.

"You enjoy being outdoors, don't you?" Tom's deep, blue eyes gazed lovingly in hers.

She shrugged her shoulders. "I do love the stillness of the woods, the grandeur of the mountains, the rippling sound of streams and lakes. Yes. I do relish being outdoors where it's restful and free to experience the miracle of creation," she said dreamily, breathing in the sovereignty of the landscape.

Tom took her hands in his, looked into her lovely flawless face, then said, "Valora, I've been wanting to talk to you alone for sometime now." He looked to the ground and breathed a sigh. After a moment of hesitation he gazed into her engaging brown eyes. She became all goose bumps with butterflies swarming around inside her stomach. Her world seemed to hush, pausing for him to speak.

"Valora, uh, I've been giving this a lot of thought and much prayer. And . . . well . . . we've known each other nearly a year now. And I, I feel there just couldn't be a more perfect combination than you and me . . . oh, Valora . . . what I'm trying to say so poorly is, I would like you to become my wife."

He looked so vulnerable. This man who stood so tall and muscular, so full of courage, and always there when she had needed him. Now he looked like a soft, pussy willow.

"My dear, sweet Tom," she touched her hand to his precious face, "I would be very honored to become your wife."

He drew her into his strong powerful arms with such a gentle embracing touch, that Valora's throbbing heart beat so loudly she seemed to hear a flourish of trumpets exploding across the sky. When their lips touched, she melted into his embrace, and the miracle of love once again enfolded two hearts into one.

Finally, he whispered, "Is there anyone I should ask for your hand in marriage?"

"Well, I guess maybe Suelena . . . or Papa Mack?"

"Do you think they will approve?" His eyes twinkled.

"I can't imagine either one saying no. You're going to be stuck with me now," she said, and he kissed her once again so tenderly.

This time Valora broke the spell. "We best be getting back to the house. I can't wait to tell Suelena."

As she started to rise from the log, he said, "You are so beautiful, Valora. I love you so very much."

"I love you, too, my darling." Three little words that mean so much when spoken in truth.

They didn't realize how rapidly the time had gone by. They hurried on back to the ranch anxious to share their news. When they entered the kitchen, they found Suelena putting the finishing touches on supper, "Where have you two been? We were getting worried about you."

"It's all my fault." Tom quickly accepted the blame.

"We just completely lost track of time. I'm so sorry, Suelena. I've got some exciting news to tell you." She looked first at Tom, as if asking for his permission, then to her sister. "Tom has asked me to marry him." The words were spoken so softly, as if a prayer.

"Oh! That's marvelous news." Suelena exuberantly hugged Valora, then Tom. "I just knew you two would be perfect for each other. I'm so very happy for you. When's the big day? Have you decided when the wedding will be?" Excitedly she asked questions, but not giving Valora time enough to answer.

"What's going on in here?" Joel came in from the other room after hearing all the commotion.

"Well, Pa, I've asked Valora to be my bride, and she said YES." His usual calm demeanor relinquished to expressions of love afire.

"I do hope you approve, Papa Mack." Valora looked at him, seeking his confirmation.

"Approve? I couldn't be happier." Joel embraced Valora, then grasped Tom's arm, shaking his hand profusely. "Congratulations, Tom. I'm very proud of you." He couldn't hide his pleasure even if he had wanted to.

"What's all the hubbub about?" Paul asked. He had heard all the hullabaloo from outside, and thought he'd better find out what he might be missing out on.

"Valora and I are getting married." There was no hesitation from Tom.

"Married! How about that! Now anytime you need some sympathy, you come to me, Valora." He pretended to punch his older brother in the arm, then gave him a big man-hug.

"It's about time. I thought maybe I was going to beat you to the altar."

"Beat me, eh?"

"Shall we tell them now, Suelena?"

Suelena had a great big smile on her lips. "Yes, I can't wait any longer."

"Well my dear family, as you know, I've been taking Suelena to school and picking her up the last few days because of the bad weather. We've been talking about what we wanted to do with out lives, and all of a sudden, yesterday she just blurted out. Suelena asked me to marry her." Paul grinned.

"Oh, Paul! That's not true." Suelena gasped and nudged him, turning a bright, cherry red.

"Nooo," Paul laughed, "I asked Suelena to marry me, and she agreed." He was beaming.

Both girls began emitting out expressions of delight, as they danced around the room, hugging each other.

"That's wonderful news. Why didn't you tell us right away?" Valora finally asked.

"We wanted to work out problems with her teaching position first," Paul answered. "For some strange reason there are some people who believe a teacher shouldn't be married," he displayed an amusing face.

"That's about the dumbest thing I've heard of," Tom replied. "What have you found out, if anything?"

"They are supposed to have a meeting this weekend to decide," Suelena sighed.

It wasn't until the following Monday morning that Suelena learned of the decision about her job situation. Although a few expressed strong beliefs about having a single schoolmarm, the majority ruled in favor of allowing their school teacher to be engaged for the rest of the school year. Since Suelena had already proven herself well-qualified, and the children highly respected her, they felt it was in the best interest of all concerned . . . for now.

"We are a progressive city, and we want to keep up with the times," one of the board members had said. But, they felt they needed to check further with the school board in Olympia before they could give a definite yes about the next school year in the fall.

Both girls expended more than a fragment of time day-dreaming nostalgic pictures of their weddings in their imaginations. Valora wanted Sarah to be in her wedding party. Suelena decided to ask Bonnie. They both desired a spring wedding with an abundance of flowers.

One evening while washing up the dishes together, Valora had an inspiration. "Why don't we have a double wedding ceremony?"

"A double wedding? That's a terrific idea. Sarah could be your bridesmaid and Bonnie could be my matron of honor. Hmm, the church is rather small. How about a garden wedding?" Suelena suggested.

"Let's have the ceremony right here on the front lawn. It has always reminded me of what the Garden of Eden must have looked like. Maybe the guys could build a trellis. We could plant some sweet, smelling honeysuckle to grow over it." Valora started landscaping the huge yard already.

"With roses!" Suelena contributed, nodding her approval. "We must have lots more roses. Oh, this sounds dreamy. Susie and Kaye could be our flower girls; the twins, our ring bearers. Who should give us away?"

"Papa Mack!" They both evoked the same thought out loud, laughing together.

After sharing their ideas with the men, while sitting around the warm fire, they all expressed their agreement. "Whatever you girls want is fine with us," they had said. Papa Mack felt honored to be chosen to represent their father. Paul wanted Sheriff Randal for his best man. Tom would ask Mark to be his best man. They felt sure he would agree, if the wedding could be in late June when his classes would be completed for the year. June would be a picture perfect month; the weather is usually nicer. If it did rain, they decided the ceremony could be moved inside, yet they would still hope for a warm sunny day.

The cold winter months merged silently into an early spring, awakening the sleeping, golden daffodils. Little gems of rainbow-colored hues of crocus could be seen squinting up into the springtime sun, and snow-white, cherry blossoms began showing their buoyant display. The girls had been busy sewing virgin-white dresses, each deciding to keep their own secret design. With the wedding drawing closer each passing day, the family cherished the rare and precious moments spent together as a family.

"What would be some profound advice you would like to share with us, Papa Mack, which helped you in your long marriage to Mattie?" Suelena asked one evening.

He thought for a moment, then said, "I could share numerous suggestions. Let's see, maybe not the first priority, but one I think very important. I believe a marriage partner should have a good sense of humor, be able to laugh at your own mistakes and not take them so seriously, or think of them as devastating, yet learn from them. Be willing to compromise. Someone once said that marriage is a fifty-fifty proposition, but sometimes you'll find that you will need to give in one hundred percent of the time. Then at other times you will receive one hundred percent in a decision. Over the long haul the percentages probably balance out that fifty-fifty.

"Also, be willing to allow your spouse to make a mistake now and then. Don't expect your loved one to always be perfect. None of us are. Be willing to say, 'I'm sorry' and mean it, even if you feel you were not in the wrong. Someone has to say those healing words first. Don't invariably wait for your partner to be the primary one to reconcile your differences, and there will be some."

He thought for a moment, then went on. "One of the special things about my Mattie, no matter how busy she may have been, she nearly always took time to freshen herself up and look her best before sitting down to the evening meal. She was such a lovely lady, not just a woman . . . but a lady. Many women live in this world, not all of them are ladies. Anyway, taking those few minutes to brush her hair or even put on a clean dress before the meal, such a little gesture, yet it gave me a feeling of being someone special to her. I think sometimes, after a couple has been married for a while, they forget their spouse enjoys looking across the table at the pretty or handsome face they married. Some women I've noticed forget how a comb or brush works wonders, or a bath, or a clean dress. Also, after a hard day of work, it's nice to enter into a clean, neat home that lovingly had been given attention by devoted caring hands. Somehow 'the work' takes on a worthwhile meaning. Just remember, it's not so difficult to catch a spouse. The real effort lies in keeping one!

"On the other side of a good marriage, a man has the same responsibilities. He should be clean about himself, either shave or keep his beard trim and neat, and let his little lady know he cares enough for her to change his clothes once in a while." His family began snickering by this time, and although Joel meant what he had said, he released an amusing facial expression too.

"And while you're smiling, give some thought to this . . . you'll find fun in taking a bath together . . . at least once in a while." He noticed the women's faces turning to shades of crimson. Joel, although serious, became amused. Then he changed the subject.

"I have something I would like you four to do for me. Tom . . . Paul . . . would you please go to your rooms and each of you bring down a pair of your pants?" They looked puzzled, yet followed their father's instructions.

Presently, they both came down the stairs with those quizzical expressions still on their faces, which turned into grins as they held their trousers out to their father. "I'd like you to give them to the girls. Now, Valora and Suelena, please go to your rooms and put on the trousers."

Promptly Suelena came down the stairs with Paul's britches rolled up several times, while hanging on to the waistband so they wouldn't fall off. Valora stumbled out of her room holding Tom's pants at her waist, the pants also rolled up so she could walk. Everyone started laughing at one another.

"All right, I want you girls to look at each other. Tom's pants do not fit Valora, and Paul's pants do not fit Suelena. You agree?" They shook their heads yes. "Remember, in every community, whether a town, a church, a business, or a family there's a need for a leader. God's intention, I believe, has forever been for the man to be the head of the house. The Bible teaches in Ephesians 5:21–22 that a wife is to be subject to her husband, which is being dependent on, to respect him, and honor him.

"In turn, the husband is the designated leader over his family, as Christ is the head of the church. And bear in mind, He loved the church enough to die for it. After God had completed His work of creation, He was pleased. But, then He saw it was not good for man to be alone, and so the Lord God caused a deep sleep to come over the first man, Adam, took one of his ribs and fashioned a woman, Eve (Genesis 2:18–22). Now, we find the woman God created was for man to love and cherish, not the man made for a woman. She was created to be a complement to her husband, to encourage him,

181

to 'complete' him. Some women can't quite comprehend what I am saying.

"When a man and a woman come to the place in their lives and find they do not want to face the challenges of life without each other, when they desire to accept the responsibilities that go along with marriage, and are prepared to establish a lifelong commitment to God, as well as one another, then it's time to join the two in the holy bonds of matrimony.

"A husband and wife should be devoted to each other, be of the same mind. In God's Book it says, 'become one.' In everything you do, consider and respect the desires and feelings of your mate. And above everything, seek God's wisdom in all things . . . every day. I believe a couple who makes God the center of their home and seeks His guidance, will have a successful and loving marriage.

"But even in the most prosperous marriages, there will be disagreements. Whenever two or more people live together, differences of opinions do arise. Don't be timid about being the first to say, 'I'm sorry.' I know I've said this before, but it's very important in any relationship. For some, those two words become so very hard to say, yet can be the unequaled prescription in a marriage. The Good Book teaches us not to let the sun set on our anger (Ephesians 4:26). We are to strive to make amends before we go to bed.

"Be gracious to one another, talk kindly to each other, respecting one another's needs or ideas. Don't go into a marriage with the idea you're going to change that other person. It rarely works. Convey to your partner in action and in words, 'I love you' . . . everyday . . . and mean them with all your heart. One of my favorite chapters in the Bible is the thirteenth chapter of First Corinthians, the 'Love' chapter. It would be good for each of you to read it often.

"Well . . . you asked me for some words of wisdom. You didn't ask for a sermon. I hope you don't get the impression

I've been preaching to you," He broke into a broad grin, they softly laughed, then he went on. "Marriage can be a very beautiful, fulfilling relationship, and I believe that is what God has intended for us. It's one that everyone needs to work at to make it survive the contentions that surely come our way. I will be praying for you every day of my life. And I want you to promise you will pray for me, as well as yourselves."

"Of course we will. And thank you, Papa Mack, for caring enough to share these beloved thoughts with us. We certainly will take them to our hearts and try our best to apply them in our marriages," Valora responded, giving Joel a big hug then kissing him on his cheek, each agreeing with what she said.

Sixteen

Each day of life can hold little glimpses of sunshine, little jewels in disguise, even if the weather is cloudy and gray. A robin sat perched on the kitchen windowsill chirping its hello. Valora just knew that little bird was the same one that came by nearly every day. When she carefully walked over to the window, it lifted its wings to the sky, as if it had done its duty of waking her up for another day. She peered out through the curtains, as they flowed in the breeze, and spied a family of quail one by one in procession strolling by. A colorful pheasant stood proud, its head held erect, straining to hear the sounds of the wilderness for friend or foe. The rich foliage and lacy ferns were uncurling their green branches. Spring, Valora decided, was her favorite time of year, except for Christmas, and autumn, and summer time. Well, she just liked living. The special time of spring is when Mother Nature steps in to scatter her seeds, doing her best to duplicate the joy of simple things, and magnify God's extravagant grace. It is evident that God enjoys beauty.

In memory's reservoir Valora recalled how her mother had loved the uncontrollable, golden dandelions. She would often say, "If they didn't grow so easily, they would be as precious as a daisy." Then she started thinking about Gruffy, their pet black bear they had freed last fall. "He must be out of hibernation by now. I wonder if he would recognize any of us?" She thought, *Maybe Sarah and the children would like to go back to Bear Lake with me and see if we can find him.*

The following Saturday, that's exactly what happened. A slight cool breeze kept the weather from being warm enough for a picnic. Still the youngsters reveled in being carefree, playing tag and trying to catch butterflies in flight, all the things that capture a child's imaginative heart. "Don't go too far off," Sarah called out to them. The deep, blue lake imitated the blue of the sky. It was calm and the lake sparkled from the sun's bright rays, as the sunlight glimmered through the budding trees. A gray squirrel jumped from one high tree limb to the next, chattering, as it seemed to fly through the air, all the while reminding them of their intrusion on its personal property.

"What a peaceful day. It's nice to escape to our favorite place now and then, just to relax and enjoy the beauties of nature. You must be getting excited about the upcoming wedding," Sarah said dreamily.

"Yes, both Suelena and I have been working rigorously on our dresses. Also, we've planted various kinds of flowers in the front yard. It's been so much fun to plan and dream. Are you going to be able to find time to make your dress?"

"Oh, yes. All I have left is to sew on the sleeves and hem it up. I really like the style you chose. It will be very pretty."

Suddenly the younger girls began screaming. All four of the children were running in the direction of the carriage, following at their heels was a small, black cub. None of them wanted to take a chance this time on angering a big, mother bear. The young women hurried the youngsters into the carriage. Immediately, a huge, black bear appeared from out of the bushes. Valora couldn't be certain if the animal might be their friend or not, but she called out his name, "Gruffy! Gruffy! Do you remember us?"

The bear slowed down its pace to a leisurely lumber towards the carriage; he raised his nose up into the air and let out a growl. At once another full-grown bear emerged, but smaller than the one making its way to the carriage. The party in the vehicle didn't know exactly what to do. Valora was having a struggle keeping the horses calm.

She called out again, "Gruffy! Gruffy! Is that you?" The larger animal ambled over to the open carriage and began sniffing at her dress. She knew then it must be Gruffy. He continued sniffing for a treat like he had become accustomed to doing when he was their pet. Valora offered the bear a cookie; he took it gently. She released a sigh and decided he must be showing off his family to his people friends. The children abandoned their fear, delighted in seeing their former pet and began to giggle, as they stretched out their hands to stroke the head of their wild, yet domesticated friend. Then the little cub came up to the vehicle, stood on his hind haunches and let out a tiny snarl, as if to say, "I wanna play, too."

The mama bear didn't appear quite so friendly. She stood off in the distance, keeping her curious eyes fixed steadily on everything taking place. After a while she let out a loud growl. The little cub hesitated, then ran towards his mama. Gruffy paused a moment, not quite ready to leave, then finally turned and strolled off into the woods with his family.

"Bye, Gruffy. Bye," the children all hollered out.

"Wasn't it exciting to see how content and proud Gruffy is? He even wanted us to meet his family," Sarah tried to smooth over the sadness that had come upon her brothers and sisters. "Just settle in your memory the privilege of being counted among his friends. Maybe we can come back and see our new family again soon," she encouraged them with her thoughtfulness. She had really accepted the role as female caretaker of the younger brothers and sisters with such tenderness and devotion since her mother had died last year. Both Valora and Suelena felt so much admiration for their mutual friend.

It was one of those nights, so still, a peaceful calm, as the McCalister family gathered around the open hearth a few days later. Joel stoked the crackling fire and stood gazing into the flickering flames for a moment. He hadn't really even comprehended why the shadows of loneliness began to besiege him; until recently did he realize why. The dread being over the day when he would be losing the intimacy of his family. Mark, still off at school, soon would be achieving his ultimate goal of serving as a physician, only God knows where. Tom and Paul were preparing for their marriages and would be moving out on their own in their immediate future, taking the girls along with them. The sadness which had been resurrecting the pangs of loneliness in his heart again paralleled the anguish he knew when Mattie died.

Momentarily, he spoke with just a touch of agonizing pain in his words, "What are some of the thoughts and plans you've been considering for your new lives, following the wedding?"

"I'm glad you asked, Pa. Suelena and I have been giving it a lot of thought, and we feel it would be wise for us to move closer to Cascadia, because of her teaching position. It appears the town council has accepted the fact she will be married," Paul began. "I've done some checking with the merchants in town. Mr. Garvey has offered me a position at the bank as bookkeeper and part-time teller. He said business is picking up and feels he will be needing some extra help by the middle of summer. I would still have time to help you with the books here at the ranch though," he quickly added with sincerity.

"Sure sounds like a good opportunity for you, son. Have you found a place to live yet?"

"There's a small two bedroom house just south of town we found for sale. It needs some work, but it shows lots of potential," Suelena voiced her excitement.

"Then that's settled. I've been wondering what kind of a

gift I could give you for a wedding present. So, if it's all right with both of you, I would like very much to make the down payment on the house, as a wedding gift from me."

"Pa, you don't have to do that. I've been saving some money and . . ."

"You use your money for furniture. I would be proud to help you get started in buying your first home," Joel said.

"Oh, Papa Mack, you're so generous. It's so exciting to think of having our own home." Suelena couldn't withhold revealing her feelings.

"That's resolved then." The father seemed relieved. "How about you, Tom and Valora? What have you been conjuring up in your minds?" A smile came across Joel's face.

"I'm not sure what you'll think about our idea, but Valora and I would like to make our home right here in the house with you," Tom answered.

"The house is so big, and I just couldn't bear to leave you here all alone." Valora directed her eyes up into his bewildered face with such a compassionate expression.

For the first time since his sons had announced their plans to wed, Joel McCalister felt an uplifting relief capture his burdened heart. Finally, he focused his glance on Valora. "My dear, sweet, little lady, those are some of the most precious words I could ever hear. But I couldn't let you do that. I'll be fine, and you two need a home of your own. You'll eventually be having a family of your own."

"Papa Mack, I love this ranch, and consider it an honor to keep on caring for this house, and you, and Tom . . . that is, if you will consent to our proposal," she said with warm affection.

"I just don't want you to have the impression that I have to be taken care of. You're more than welcome to live on the ranch with me. But there can only be one head of the house, and I've held that position for quite some time now. I don't think I could relinquish that role, even to my oldest son just yet." He was trying to be realistic about the situation.

"We don't want you to feel our intention is one of taking over, or that you have to accept our proposal," Tom interceded. "We would like each of us to seek God's direction in helping us come to the appropriate decision for all concerned."

"And Papa Mack, if you'd rather we found our own place to make a home, please tell us. You've been like a father to me, and to Suelena. I love you very much and we only want what will be best for you, as well as for Tom and I," Valora shared.

"Well, sooner or later there will be the sounds of little feet running up and down the stairs." A wave of tender feeling began to move the soul of Joel; the more he dwelt on the idea, the more his facial expression could not hide the satisfaction he was embracing.

"Are you absolutely sure you want to continue to live here with me?" His disbelief became apparent.

"Dear Papa Mack, please know how much we both love you. We will do our best to make the transition as uninterrupted to your way of life as much as possible. I've lived here in this wonderful home over a year now. I'm confident that we can continue to live under the same roof with the same expressions of love we have been sharing this past year. And as you have told us before, sincere love is eternal. It doesn't die. With God's help we will make it work."

"Hmm, the hour is late. Let's sleep on our decision. If I discover God directing us down this path, and I find peace in whatever God reveals in my soul, I will share it with you," Joel concluded.

The following evening after supper, Valora and Tom decided to go for a walk. The spring days were getting longer; the weather mild, with a fragrance of purple lilacs seeping into the air along the pathway they chose, where tall hollyhocks grow wild. Pink-tipped apple blossoms could be viewed bursting out in bud in preparation for their task of producing succulent fruit in the late summer. Busy bees wasted no time buzzing from one dainty flower to the next, while capturing the sweet nectar and carrying out God's plan of pollination of the fruit tress. Hushing sounds of the forest nearby, except for a trill from a wild bird now and then, set the stage for a quiet esthetic evening made for two people in love.

Enraptured by the miracles of God's unique gifts and the radiance of the inner feeling that stirred within their hearts, just a gentle touch to her cheek energized a quiver through Valora's body.

"Are you cold?" Tom whispered, as he drew her close to him and leaned against a tree.

Valora gazed up into his exquisite, blue eyes that reflected sparkles of sunlight like rock crystals dangling in the sun. She smiled and shook her head, no. Their eyes lingered on each other for a caressing moment. When their lips touched, the rest of the world wandered off into a distant land. New love is so precious, so pure, a treasured gift given us by our Creator above. A sacred gift that grows more deeply rooted through the years, when nurtured with respect, tender words, thoughtfulness, faithfulness, and desiring the welfare each for the other . . . resulting in a neverending love affair.

After a while they wandered along a trail probably derived from the untamed animals that inhabited the primitive woods, as they amble their way through the under brush. They found a clearing and sat down on a carpet of soft, fir needles beside a clear, reflecting stream that toppled over a bed of jagged stones forming a tiny waterfall. Branches from the towering evergreens gathered rays from the sun's shine, inspiring the green leaves of shamrocks to grow at their base. Valora found a stem with four heart-shaped leaves, picked it and proclaimed, "This is our good luck charm. Let's make a wish and see if it comes true."

"All my dreams and more have already come true, since you came into my life, Valora. Women are not that plentiful out here in the wilds of the Washington territory. You're over and above what I ever imagined, or even hoped I would find . . . you are so lovely, and share so many of the same interests I enjoy." He brushed a lock of shimmering, red hair back from her eyes and kissed her once again, so tenderly her heart felt like it was flying up to join the cottony clouds of white touched off with tinges of sunset.

Time had swiftly drifted away unnoticed until now. High overhead hung the bright, yellow moon, creating a romantic essence, as it spread its twilight across the darkening sky with stardust falling like rain. The sun was wearily sending off beautiful shades of coral across the realm above.

"We better be heading back to the house before they send out a search party for us, my little darling." Tom touched her nose gently with his finger. She grabbed it and kissed the tips of each finger, then wrinkled her nose a little, and he smiled his glorious grin. Neither one not really wanting to surrender these treasured moments alone together in their silent, secret place.

Earlier that day, Paul and Suelena had checked in town about the ownership of the house they were interested in purchasing. They found the price reasonable and confirmed an early appointment to meet the owners the following day, when the papers could be drawn up. Arrangements would then be set forth to take occupation of the house by the end of the month, making it available to conduct any needed repairs in hopes of having it ready to move into immediately following the wedding.

Suelena's enthusiasm was contagious, as she shared her

plans and decorating ideas with her sister. Tom offered his help to Paul, with assistance from their father to build furniture from the money Paul had been saving. Joel told them they could have Paul's bedroom furniture he had crafted several years ago, if they would like it. Suelena was thrilled with the offer of the large poster bed made from hardwood and a matching dresser, both intricately carved with floral designs. Joel truly showed the ability of a craftsman with his hands.

It wasn't until the week's end that Joel mentioned the conversation he shared earlier in the week with Tom and Valora. Starting the dialogue, he said, "I've been meditating a lot about the discussion we had the other night. The conclusion I've been led to believe is this: if you, Tom and Valora feel agreeable, I'm willing to try out your suggestion of making your home here with me. What I would like, if you find it suitable, is for you to claim the rooms upstairs as your own. We can move Mark's belongings downstairs into the room Valora now has, for as long as he wants to come home. I'm sure he won't mind. I'll keep my bedroom as such, and the rest of the house will, of course, be for all of us to share as a family just as we've been doing. The first thing we need to accomplish though is to get Paul and Suelena's home in top notch condition before the wedding."

"That's marvelous news, Pa. We'll give it our best, and if at anytime we determine it is not working out, we will make a change," Tom stated.

"I'm sure we'll be very happy together," Valora said with satisfaction, giving Papa Mack one of her loving hugs.

Seventeen

A tranquility and contentment had dispelled any tension that had arisen in the family, since the decision became known that Tom and Valora would share the lovely log home with Joel following their wedding. Valora went about the household duties with a song on her lips and she even overheard Papa Mack humming some of his favorite tunes now and then.

As soon as the papers were signed on the property Paul and Suelena had purchased, permission was granted for them to start their remodeling project, which the whole family took part in. The one-storied house located on the south end of town would be walking distance to the school where Suelena taught. The nice sized yard had become overgrown with tall untrammeled grass. A large apple tree brightened up the yard in full blossoms on one side of the building and a cherry tree was finishing blooming still equally as lovely on the other. Several rose bushes by the front porch growing in amongst the weeds, were beginning to show buds. A picket fence lined the front yard, crying out the need to be strengthened and repaired with a board or two, and also needed to be spruced up with a coat of paint.

Inside, the snug cottage pleaded for restoration of plaster here and there, as well as freshening up with paint. The chamber they would be using for their master bedroom proved a good size. Suelena had already arranged in her thoughts Paul's bedroom furniture in just the perfect places. A second bedroom Suelena claimed for her sewing and study room, at least for now. The living room appeared large, as was the kitchen that housed an abundance of cupboards and a space for a nice sized table and chairs. "Big enough to have the McCalister clan over for dinner often," she proclaimed.

While the men settled on the carpentry work, the girls decided to tackle the yard and endeavor to make it more presentable. They each took a flower garden on either side of the front porch and proceeded to weed the flower beds. Valora declared, while taking time to glance around the yard, "I think we ought to borrow a couple of Judsons' sheep to mow the grass." Suelena laughingly agreed with her.

All of a sudden Valora let out a blood-curdling scream. While pulling up a weed, somehow she came up with the tail end of a large snake. So startled was she, that all the frightened lady could do was stand there holding onto the wiggling reptile by its tip end, until Suelena ran to see what happened. As soon as she saw the snake, she yelled, "Throw it!"

Valora did. Yep! It landed right on Suelena. Now they were both screaming out in uncontrollable shrills, causing the men to come running out of the house, "What in the world is going on out here?" Tom hollered.

"It's a snake!" Valora shrieked.

Tom grabbed the slimy reptile. "It's just a garter snake, honey. It won't harm you. Actually, they're good to have around, 'cause they catch the insects and help keep them under control."

"Well, I don't want any! I don't like those sneaky things around here!" Suelena was nearly in hysterics.

Paul was finally able to calm her down, but said, "I'm sorry, love. They do live around these parts. Just try to be more cautious when you work in the flower garden. They're probably as much afraid of you as you are them."

"I don't think so!" Suelena declared, with Valora readily shaking her head in an agreeable expression.

194

"If I would have lived in the Garden of Eden, that apple never would have been eaten, 'cause I never would have talked to that dirty ol' snake!" Suelena went on.

Paul decided to stay outside to take time to mend the fence. Soon the sisters were calmly spreading white paint over each board meticulously, bringing it back to life again.

When the broken window panes were replaced and needed repairs finished on the outside of the building, the outer surface of the house was covered in white. The men painted the higher, more difficult areas to reach. The women painted the lower exterior and distinctive, ornate trim.

One day while they diligently worked, Sarah came by with a picnic basket full of sandwiches, fried chicken, cookies and cold apple cider. "I thought you might like to take a little break from all your hard work," she smiled, never too busy to help out her friends.

"Sarah, you are such a jewel." Valora gave her a squeeze, and soon the three young women and three men (since Joel had decided to join them and found a project to work on), started chattering over the welcome treat. Eventually the men went back inside to their respective projects.

"Would you care to see inside and inspect our crowning achievements?" Suelena asked their friend, as a smile of pride came into view. "There's still much work to be done. But, this way you can see the 'before and after' of our labor," she stated.

Suelena tried opening the front door. It didn't want to budge, so she pushed on it with all of her strength. As she did, Paul let out a yell, at the same time he and his ladder toppled over, the paint bucket he had been holding to paint the ceiling with tipped over and fell. The pail just missed Suelena's head . . . but not the paint.

"Ohhh!" she let out a squeal, covering her mouth with a hand. "I'm so sorry, Paul! Are you hurt? I didn't realize you were there," she tried her best to apologize. All the while the paint flowed down her hair and face, covering her clothing. There didn't seem to be much of her apparel left untouched with the splattering of the white liquid.

Sarah tried hard to keep her composure, by constraining her mouth with her hands. Tom, however, began to chuckle, then Valora, and pretty soon everyone had to release their emotions. No more chuckles, just plain out-and-out laughter. Joel managed to rescue Paul from under the ladder to see if he may have been injured. Instead of injury, he was doubled over from laughing at the creative expression of dismay on his bride-to-be's face, and yet feeling sorry for her in such a distraught condition.

It took a while for Suelena to clean herself up. The girls did find an old water pump out behind the house by the kitchen door. After some priming, the water finally spouted out of the ancient beauty and Suelena bathed herself off as much as she could. Her emotions caused her to "sense a feeling much like that of a drowned toad," she decided.

"I think we've accomplished enough for today," Joel ultimately announced. "Let's all go home to our haven of rest." It didn't surprise him when no objection could be heard from the suggestion.

Except for the wasted paint, the rest of the restoration project seemed to continue rather smoothly. Getting Paul and Suelena's house in good living condition took some hours. Nevertheless, it remained well worth the task. New boards and paint can cover up a multitude of nicks and flaws. New windows replaced a few broken ones. The picket fence in the front yard sparkled with white-wash, helping to spruce up the former ram-shackled dwelling. Now the house took on a charm, just offering to be hospitable to its new tenants.

A floral carpet had been purchased for the living area. Carefully hung lace curtains flowed gracefully from the open windows, as they aired out the fresh paint odor. Joel offered Paul and Suelena the opportunity to explore the attic of the McCalister home for anything they might want to use in their new residence.

They promptly responded to his offer and delighted in spending hours of enjoyment rummaging through numerous boxes of accumulated memories, truly a browser's paradise. Old tin pictures of the boys as youngsters were discovered, one being a photograph of the entire family, although discolored from the fire years ago. Mark was a baby being held by a lovely young Mattie, as she sat in a straight-backed chair. Joel stood behind her, stiff and tall sporting a thick mustache, wearing his hair parted down the middle. Paul was nearly three, and Tom must have been about six. Everyone had such a serious expression, without a hint of a smile on their faces.

In other pictures the men always appeared stern, several with long beards. Many of the women stood clothed in fancy dresses. Some turned for a side profile to show off the bustles that puffed out the back of the dress.

Paul and Suelena decided to frame the picture of the young McCalister family to hang on a wall in their refurbished home. She felt sure Valora would appreciate seeing the pictures they had discovered, too. Both girls had often wished they had some family portraits of their mother and father from a bygone era.

Old paintings of beautifully depicted floral gardens, unique tapestries, intricately crocheted and dainty tatted doilies, old but still durable dishes, and other collections and keepsakes rich in memories were also found to add a touch of endearment that makes a house a home.

Furniture would be their next project. With help from Annie at the general store, the young couple ordered the latest style in iron cook stoves through the catalog. They chose a wooden stove described with a color of baked-on pale, yellow enamel housing a nice sized oven, and featuring two warming ovens attached to the top. One side of the flat surface would be used for frying foods and heating the cooking pots. They also ordered an ice box to match, hoping the new appliances would arrive soon after the wedding.

In the meantime the men, under Joel's expertise, diligently set to work crafting a large, beautifully detailed table and chair set out of oak for the space in the kitchen. With meticulous workmanship the framework for a sofa and two chairs was skillfully assembled, giving attention to detail and classic artistry. The girls sewed well-padded cushions for each. By the time the furniture was completed, the nuptial date was just around the corner; and Mark should be coming in from college any day now.

Just for the fun of it, Valora and Suelena kept their wedding dress designs a secret from each other. Sarah spent as much time as she could giving assistance with their fittings and hemming of the dresses, helping make it a labor of fun and pleasure for each one.

Time for the wedding day drew near to its climax. It had been a rainy week, so both of the girls took advantage of the evening hours sewing last minute stitches on their dresses.

Excitement filled the environment around town as well, since talk of the marriage spread from friends to neighbors. Most had never been to a double wedding before, and being a garden ceremony the fascination increased.

Tom and Paul had built a large trellis at one corner of the huge yard earlier in the year, when the girls decided they wanted a garden wedding. Soon after their carpentry work had been completed, Joel had planted a honeysuckle vine at its footing, which was interlacing itself around the sturdy white, latticed work, while releasing a sweet aroma from its blossoms. On either side of the trellis grew a row of various shades of roses. Pale pink, floral clusters donned several rhododendron bushes, taking their places behind the fragrant roses. A white, petaled dogwood bloomed in seclusion now and then in the distance among the shiny green-leafed madrona trees with red bark, scrub oak and towering firs. Snow-covered and proud Mt. Rainier could be seen in the discrete background behind the trellis, enhancing the scenery. The velvet green grass grew tall because of the rainy weather. The rain had also encouraged a variety of flowers to give life to an abundance of buds in waiting.

The ancient tradition of having something old, something new, something borrowed, something blue was becoming somewhat of a jigsaw puzzle. The new, borrowed and blue were easy enough. Suelena had decided to wear the emerald necklace Valora had given her as a gift when she first came, and Valora the Christmas necklace from Tom. Valora borrowed a lovely bracelet from Sarah. Suelena borrowed the wedding veil Bonnie had worn at her wedding. Both had made blue garters. But the "old" remained the problem, until Joel mentioned to Valora, "What about your band of gold?"

Valora had never removed her mother's circlet of gold from her finger, the one she had found in the fire . . . it seemed like ages ago now. The precious golden band had just become a part of her being. "Yes!" she exclaimed, "how could I have forgotten about Mama's ring? I suppose I should change it to my other hand," she grinned.

"Please, let me put the band on your other finger." Tom, with adoration, reached for her hand. He peered intently into her vulnerable eyes and gently slid the plain, golden band from off her finger and placed the special remembrance on her right hand. Tears began to well up in her dark eyes. He soothingly wiped them away, then kissed her softly.

"Thank you, Tom. I don't think I could ever have removed the ring. I wouldn't have wanted anyone else but you take it off." Valora smiled lovingly at her fiancé.

199

Joel left the room and came right back with a tiny box in his hand. "Paul, I'd like for you to place this on Suelena's finger. This wedding band belonged to your mother."

"Oh, Papa Mack, what a beautiful gesture, but I couldn't accept your precious keepsake." Suelena looked astonished.

"Mattie would want me to give it to you. And I know you'll cherish it as much as I do."

Paul took the golden band and placed it on Suelena's third finger of her right hand, then lovingly kissed her, giving her one of his affectionate smiles.

"This is almost a ceremony in itself," Valora spoke in deepest praise, capturing the sentiment of such a unique occasion. "Thank you, Papa Mack, for being so thoughtful. We do love you so, and I hope we can make you proud to be your daughter-in-laws."

"You both already have, although my gift pales next to your gift of love. And best of all, the Good Lord is never outdone in His generosity, and will surely bless your marriages . . . with little ones running through this house coming to see me," he expressed with light-hearted laughter. Everyone joined in his sportive humor.

Eighteen

The middle of June finally arrived, bringing forth whisper soft, fluffy clouds floating slowly by. Mark had been home a week and everyone was anticipating the ultimate joy of such a meaningful event this particular day would bring. By early afternoon throngs of people started to arrive for the wedding, trampling on the carpet of lush grass, and exclaiming over the panoramic pageant of floral colors in a profusion of bloom. God had smiled down and warmed the celestial, blue sky with a radiant, golden sun. Honeybees busily buzzed among the purple clover growing nearby. Dainty gems of wild buttercups burst into yellow blooms. Delicate Queen Anne's Lace was attracting the fluttering butterfly with its exotic wings. There is that once in a while when everything seems to go just perfect. Today appeared to be the day, at least the McCalister family and two lovely ladies felt optimistic.

The heavy, upright piano had been rolled out onto the porch; melodies of love began to fill the air from the church pianist. Borrowed chairs and benches facing the trellis quickly filled to capacity with youngsters sprawled on the grass laden with colorful quilts to sit on. The children poked fun at each other and giggled, while their parents both tried to keep them under control and visit at the same time.

Without delay, at two o'clock the minister took his place in front of the lattice structure. Joining him next came Tom, then Paul, both looking extremely handsome in their dark suits and white, ruffled shirts with high stiff collars and ascot ties. Mark, as best man for Tom, escorted the exquisite Sarah down the aisle, serving as maid of honor for Valora. She wore a full length, pale pink dress of ruffles caught in the back by a large bow, forming a bustle. The short sleeves were dainty and puffy.

Next in the procession strolled Bonnie, the matron of honor for Suelena, looking charming in her matching pink dress. She was escorted by the sheriff, Bob Randal, wearing a suit, which he felt very uncomfortable in. He managed to give in and suffer for his friend, being Paul's best man, but he refused to wear a ruffled shirt. The twins, David and Daniel, each followed the party carrying small lacy white ruffled pillows with the rings attached by pink bows. Daniel happened to trip over an untied shoestring, but managed to keep from falling. He did, however, stoop to tie his shoe, then the procession moved on.

Susie and Kaye each wore matching pink ruffled dresses similar to the attending young women, only ankle length with complementing pink pantalets. Both little girls carried a decorated basket of rose petals, which they tossed toward their fascinated audience. Kaye, the youngest, paused to wave at her daddy, Mr. Judson, while he proudly smiled and whispered for her to keep on moving.

And last, walking slowly and carefully while descending the stairs of the porch and wearing a nervous grin on his face came the proud Joel McCalister, looking very handsome and fashionable in his dark suit. The congregation of guests arose to a standing position in honor, when the pianist played the special chord. On each arm Joel escorted two very lovely brides down the aisle, as the three strolled on past the captivated audience.

Valora wore a long flowing pure white dress layered with ruffles and swags of lace, gathering in to a point at her tiny waist in front, and forming a bustle of drapery and bows down her back. A scalloped laced neckline showed off the emerald necklace perfectly. The straight lace sleeves delicately flounced at the elbow with ruffle laced edges. Her shimmering auburn hair was fashioned on top of her head in curls with several ringlets flowing down to one side. The long lace veil covered her smiling, yet nervous features.

Suelena's dress of pure white satin flowed long and full over her tall thin frame with a much smaller bustle in back; the skirt being edged with a pleated ruffle. The high neckline set off by a ruffle of floral lace, displayed her emerald necklace with elegance. The straight fitting sleeves sewed of the same delicate floral fabric had cuffs edged in dainty pleated ruffles. Her dark brown hair flowed loosely down her back in curls, covered with the lovely lace veil she had borrowed from Bonnie, which matched her dress with perfection.

After each had taken their place in front of the congregation, the minister began to speak: "My dear friends, holy and significant is this sacred hour as devoted hearts have come together on such a glorious day, asking God to bless these two couples in the enchanting ties of this holiest estate of matrimony. Excluding all sacred ceremonies, the marriage ceremony exists as the most important and honorable step a man and a woman will pledge together. Marriage is both a civil and a divine contract between a man, a woman, and God. Our Heavenly Father instituted and ordained that a man should leave his father and mother and cleave unto his wife from the time Adam and Eve were given to each other in the Garden of Eden (Genesis 2:24). May the institution of marriage and divine appointment never be entered into lightly, but discreetly and sincerely, being a lifelong commitment until in death you part.

"Our Bible teaches us that the husband is to love his wife as Christ loved His church, insomuch as He gave His life for it (Ephesians 5:21–32). The wife is to honor and respect her

203

husband. The Bible, in the book of Psalms (132:9), speaks of white as being the symbol of purity . . . so should a bride be presented to her husband, a virgin of purity. Thus the two, husband and wife, forsake all others. No longer will they be two individuals, but become one flesh: one in thought, one in hope, and one in all concerns of their lives together.

"Each of you have come today declaring your desire to be united in marriage," he smiled at the two couples. "At this time I request the one who is giving permission for these young ladies to be united with these young men to speak his approval."

Joel had been standing beside the girls and quickly replied, "With my deepest sincerity, I give my permission." He then stepped back and took an empty seat on the front row of chairs.

"Upon Joel McCalister's consent, and being assured there are no legal, moral, or religious barriers to keep from the consecrated union, I now ask each couple to join your right hands together.

"Thomas James McCalister and Paul Steven McCalister, in taking the woman you hold by the right hand to become your lawful wedded wife, before God and all these witnesses present here today, do you promise to love her with all of your heart, to honor and cherish her in that relationship, comfort her whether in sickness or in health, in difficulties or strife, and leaving all others willingly receive only her as your wife by being a true and faithful husband as long as you both shall live?"

"I do."

"I do."

"Valora Edith Dillon and Suelena Elaine Dillon, in taking the man you hold by the right hand to be your lawful wedded husband, before God and all these witnesses present today, do you promise to love him with all of your heart, to honor and cherish him in that relationship, comforting him whether in sickness or in health, in difficulties or strife, and leaving all others cling only unto him by being a true and faithful wife so long as you both shall live?"

"Oh, yes I do."

"And, I do."

The minister untied the ribbon from the pillow Daniel stood holding and picked up the ring Tom had chosen for Valora. Holding it for all to see, he said, "As a symbol of the neverending love you have promised one to another, I hold in my hand this, *a band of gold*. For many years the circlet has been utilized to seal important covenants. A reigning monarch made use of the great seal fixed upon a ring, and with its stamp transferred his sign of imperial authority to any document. The circular band was usually created from gold, the most prized of jewels. A precious metal considered remarkable for its beautiful, yellow color, density, and freedom from rust or tarnish. From such a unique substance should also a marriage be formed. A circle of love that grows with an unending length. A sincere love inspired by the presence of God; one of beauty and happiness; one of which will not rust or tarnish when poverty, sickness, or troubles may darken your door; one that's on fire with devotion for one another.

"With such a symbolic and precious token of pure and abiding qualities of the ideal state of marriage, do you, Tom, give this ring to Valora as a token and total commitment of your enduring love for her?"

"Yes, I do." He lovingly gazed into her eyes.

"Valora, will you accept this band of gold as a token and commitment of Tom's love for you and wear the ring as a token and total commitment of your neverending love for Tom?"

"Yes, with all my heart," she promised with tears of love flowing down her lovely cheeks.

Nearly the same words were spoken between Paul and Suelena.

"Now, please rejoin your right hands. Having made your pledge of faith in, and love to each other, and having sealed these solemn and holy vows of matrimony by giving and receiving of the rings in all they symbolize, I have acted under the authority given me by the Washington Territory, and in asking God's most divine approval, I pronounce you husbands and wives in the presence of our Holy Father and those assembled witnesses here today. May everyone in attendance realize you have just experienced a holy and lasting covenant, which shall ever remain sacred. And what God has joined together, may no man ever separate. Let us now bow our heads in prayer. And we who are married, may we each bring to memory and recommit our own vows of love for our spouses." Then the minister led in prayer.

"My dear friends, it gives me extraordinary pleasure to introduce to you the Mr. and Mrs. Thomas James McCalister and the Mr. and Mrs. Paul Steven McCalister. You may now kiss your brides."

As the piano began to play the recessional hymn, Tom and Valora, then Paul and Suelena walked down the aisle with expressions of loving radiance on their faces. Everyone began cheering and wishing them well. Other instrumentalists joined the pianist and the exhilarating music intensified the flow. Dancing and chattering livened up the festivities. Each one took their turn congratulating the couples and wishing them happiness. Food was plentiful and merriment abundant. It appeared the entire community of Cascadia had shown up for the wedding and were enjoying every minute of the celebration.

When the time came for the guests to leave, all the single ladies gathered in front of the porch, each one hoping to catch one of the bridal bouquets. Suelena turned her back to the line of young hopefuls and threw her nosegay of flowers. Sheriff Randal happened to amble by at that moment, unaware of what was going on, and automatically reached up and caught the flying object, not really realizing his intrusion.

"Ohh, that's not fair!" The girls all complained loudly.

The sheriff turned crimson with embarrassment, as the young girls chided him.

Valora called out, "Wait! I still have mine to throw." She turned her back and tossed the dainty flowers. This time Bonnie caught the bouquet.

Everyone joined in laughing and teasing the sheriff, trying their best to get even by embarrassing him all the more with good-natured ridicule. "We know who's getting married next!" Both Bonnie and Bob Randal looked at each other and grinned sheepishly.

Epilogue

The McCalister ranch has experienced some minor changes as the year swiftly passed by. Valora found some interesting items in the attic, bringing to mind loving memories to Joel's recollections. A little rocking horse he had made, which all three of his sons had played on as small children, had been brought to life again with a fresh coat of paint and new yarn added for its mane and tail. The refurbished horse now found its place in front of the hearth. Valora also finished painting a cradle the boys each had slept in for the new arrival due any day now.

Several friends and family had been invited for supper. Valora did her best to get the housework finished and dinner ready before everyone was to arrive. This was going to be a celebration for their first wedding anniversary, and she wanted everything to be perfect. Tom came in a little early from his chores to check to see if Valora needed any help in the preparations.

"Is there anything I can do to help you, love?" he offered. "You look tired."

"I'm fine. Everyone should be here soon." She smiled and kissed him on the cheek.

Looking out the window, she could see a horse and buggy coming down the road, followed close behind was another wagon. "Here they come now."

Along with Paul and Suelena rode Bob and Bonnie, who had married during the year. Right behind the carriage was Mark, who had gone after Sarah. Soon, Valora had lots of help putting the finishing touches to the dinner. Everyone brought along a favorite dish to add to Valora's menu. The table looked elegant as usual, and everyone enjoyed a grand time conversing through the meal, gathering up all the latest news. Suelena enjoyed her teaching job, and Paul felt very pleased with his position at the bank.

At a lull in the conversation, Mark stood up and clanged his glass with a spoon. "Ah, um, ladies and gentlemen . . . I would like to have your attention please." He grinned. "Sarah and I have an announcement to make. We made a decision today. We've decided to plan an August wedding, and would like you to be the first to hear the good news."

The girls all squealed and hugged each other. The men congratulated Mark. Then Joel asked somewhat concerned, "You're still going to finish your schooling, aren't you?"

"Oh, sure, Pa. I just don't want to go back to Seattle without Sarah beside me. I'm going to talk with her Pa tonight, when I take her home. We feel her brothers and sisters are old enough now to take on more responsibilities, so I hope he'll empathize with our decision."

"While we're making announcements, we also have one we'd like to share," Paul stated. He looked lovingly at his wife. "Suelena and I are going to have a child!"

"That's wonderful news, too," Valora said.

"When I get over my morning sickness, I'm sure I'll agree with you." Suelena scrunched a face.

While talking about Sarah's wedding plans and the new baby, the women cleaned the kitchen. The men had retired to the living room to spread their yarns.

Bonnie noticed Valora grab her stomach. "Are you all right, Valora?" she asked in concern.

"I just had a sharp pain! Oh! There's another one. I've been having them off and on all evening, but I think they're getting sharper and closer."

"We'd better get you to bed. Tom! Would you come here, please?" Bonnie called.

Tom ran into the kitchen. "What's wrong? Valora! Are you all right?" He sounded and looked so worried.

"She'll be fine, but she needs to go to bed," Bonnie reassured him. "Suelena, would you find some clean cloths, and Sarah, put on some water to heat, please?"

"Let's put her in Mark's room downstairs." Joel came in to see if he could be of help.

Tom picked Valora up and carried her to the bedroom. On the way she had another contraction, causing the usually self-controlled Tom much alarm.

"Mark, it appears you and I will need to help Valora deliver this baby," Bonnie announced. "I don't believe this little one will wait much longer."

The rest of the family waited nervously by the fireside. Tom paced the floor, wanting so badly to help his wife, but didn't know what to do but pray that everything would go well. Valora's cries of pain could be heard by her family for a couple hours before the delivery actually came.

Eventually Bonnie came out of the bedroom holding a little bundle in her arms and a loving smile on her face. "Would you like to see what you have here?" she asked Tom, who was staring at her, then at the tiny object in her hands.

"What do we have, a boy or a girl?" Tom asked anxiously.

"A sweet, little girl with lots of dark, reddish hair. Here, Tom, you want to hold her?"

"Uh, she's so tiny. I don't want to drop her." His voice was obviously nervous and a little fearful.

"She won't break, big brother." Mark came out of the bedroom about that time with a big grin. "Carry her in and see Valora. She's asking for you."

"Is she all right?"

"She's a real trouper. She did just fine." His brother looked pleased.

Tom accepted the baby from Bonnie very timidly. The tiny newborn opened her eyes, then went back to sleep in her daddy's arms. He carried her in to Valora's bedside. She looked pale and exhausted, but she began to smile as her little family entered the room, "Are you terribly disappointed it wasn't a boy?" She looked sorrowful.

"Oh, no. She's beautiful. I hope she grows up looking just like her lovely mother." Tom kissed his wife, then laid the precious gift of life God had blessed them with down beside her mother. "What shall we name her?"

"I know we had a boy's name picked out, but if it's all right with you, I've been thinking about naming her Julie Matilda McCalister," Valora suggested.

"That pleases me just fine," Tom readily agreed, looking down at his wife and daughter, filled with love.

Just then they heard a knock on the door. "May I come in?" Joel was at the door.

"Come in, Pa. Come meet my new family."

Joel walked over to the bed, kissed Valora on the forehead and touched the baby's cheek gently rubbing it with his finger. "A little girl, huh?" He inspected his first grandchild.

"Yes, Papa Mack. Tom and I just gave her a name. We've decided to name her Julie Matilda McCalister."

Tears came to the eyes of the husky gentleman, as his heart filled with emotion. "That's a lovely name, Valora, just lovely."

And Life Goes On . . .